Get Your
Coventry Romances
Home Subscription NOW

And Get These
4 Best-Selling Novels
FREE:

LACEY
by Claudette Williams

THE ROMANTIC WIDOW
by Mollie Chappell

HELENE
by Leonora Blythe

THE HEARTBREAK TRIANGLE
by Nora Hampton

A Home Subscription! It's the easiest and most convenient way to get every one of the exciting Coventry Romance Novels! . . .And you get 4 of them FREE!

You pay nothing extra for this convenience: there are no additional charges. . .you don't even pay for postage! Fill out and send us the handy coupon now, and we'll send you 4 exciting Coventry Romance novels absolutely FREE!

SEND NO MONEY, GET THESE
FOUR BOOKS
FREE!

C0582

MAIL THIS COUPON TODAY TO:
COVENTRY HOME
SUBSCRIPTION SERVICE
6 COMMERCIAL STREET
HICKSVILLE, NEW YORK 11801

YES, please start a Coventry Romance Home Subscription in my name, and send me FREE and without obligation to buy, my 4 Coventry Romances. If you do not hear from me after I have examined my 4 FREE books, please send me the 6 new Coventry Romances each month as soon as they come off the presses. I understand that I will be billed only $9.00 for all 6 books. There are no shipping and handling nor any other hidden charges. There is no minimum number of monthly purchases that I have to make. In fact, I can cancel my subscription at any time. The first 4 FREE books are mine to keep as a gift, even if I do not buy any additional books.

For added convenience, your monthly subscription may be charged automatically to your credit card.

☐ Master Charge   ☐ Visa
    42101   **42101**

Credit Card #_____

Expiration Date_____

Name_____
                   (Please Print)
Address_____

City _____State _____Zip _____

Signature_____

☐ Bill Me Direct Each Month **40105**
Publisher reserves the right to substitute alternate FREE books. Sales tax collected where required by law. Offer valid for new members only. Allow 3-4 weeks for delivery. Prices subject to change without notice.

Golden Barrier

BY

Mira Stables

FAWCETT COVENTRY • NEW YORK

GOLDEN BARRIER

This book contains the complete text of the original hardcover
edition.

Published by Fawcett Coventry Books, CBS Educational and
Professional Publishing, a division of CBS Inc., by arrange-
ment with Robert Hale Limited

ISBN: 0-449-50289-9

Printed in the United States of America

First Fawcett Coventry printing: May 1982

10 9 8 7 6 5 4 3 2 1

Golden Barrier

ONE

"Some wretched brat who is coming to Miss Fotherby's," said Lady Emma Dorsey crossly. A mutinous pout spoiled the curve of her pretty little mouth, but at sixteen she no longer feared the nursery threat that such grimaces would have a lasting effect on her beauty. "Mama says we are both to stay at home and do the polite," she went on, with a sly grin for her brother's disgusted face.

"What, me, too?" he demanded indignantly. And then, more thoughtfully, "How old is she?"

"Oh—twelve or thirteen, I suppose," returned his sister indifferently.

Lord Thomas's brief spurt of interest died. "No sport to be had there," he growled sullenly.

"Sixteen or seventeen, now, would be more like it."

Emma regarded him curiously. He was a well grown lad for his fifteen years, heavily built and full-fleshed. She wondered how much substance lay behind his frequent references to adventures in the petticoat line. He boasted a good deal, but she could see little in his disposition or his rather undistinguished countenance to appeal to a feminine fancy. As a brother he was something of a bully, with several unpleasant ways of taking his revenge if he suspected his sister of having tattled to those in authority about his doings. She hastened to appease him now, lest he should think that Mama's behest was any of her doing.

"It's no bread and butter of mine," she said firmly. "I'd never even heard of the chit until Mama called me into her dressing room. Katherine Martenhays. Some connection of Lady Julia Somersby's; but by what I could make out, her Papa's not quite the thing. Odiously wealthy, so he's probably a Cit or a vulgar mushroom. The thing is that it's our Papa who's behind this show of gracious hospitality. I daresay he wants to borrow money off Mr. Martenhays or perhaps to sell him something. Which means there can be no getting out of it. It won't do to put Papa all on end. But we needn't really trouble ourselves over-much. We can show her the grounds and the maze and take her round the stables—that sort of thing. It's only for one afternoon."

"And the last afternoon of the holidays," grumbled her brother. "What's more, I'd planned to go over to Nick's. He's got a new ferret and we were going to try it out. I've better things to do than to be dancing attendance on a nursery party. You'll manage very well without me."

"Mama said both of us," reminded his sister. "She's bound to ask. If you want to wheedle a good tip out of her when you go off tomorrow, you'll pay heed to her wishes."

Lord Thomas swore, with a fluency and force that denoted a long and close association with his father's stable hands, and a total lack of consideration for feminine ears. His sister was unmoved.

"She'll be here about two o'clock," she told him calmly.

Lord Thomas had a bright idea. "Why don't we all ride over to Nick's?" he demanded. "We can put the wench up on old Dobbs. Even a schoolgirl could hardly fall off him. Not that I'd care if she did. But I'm damned if I see wasting the last bit of freedom between here and Christmas."

Emma hesitated. She was not in the least interested in ferrets or rabbiting, but she had a distinct tendre for handsome Nick Nevison, the innkeeper's son.

"She won't be dressed for riding," she temporised, "but perhaps I could lend her my old habit—the one that I've outgrown. I could smuggle that and my new one down to the stables and we can change in the harness room. You must keep guard for us. I wouldn't mind doing that. I must say it would be deadly dull just strolling in the grounds all afternoon. But remember, not a word to Mama. She doesn't approve of my being about the inn so much. I'll volunteer to conduct our guest to the stables and say that I've arranged to meet you there."

The prospective guest was looking forward to the afternoon with sentiments that would have been appropriate in one who had been condemned to the torture chamber. Aunt Julia— who was actually a cousin of her Mama's—had announced in her brisk, 'no nonsense' voice that it would be a good thing to get upon terms with Emma Dorsey before they met at school.

"Not that she will come much in your way. She is one of the older girls, of course. I should think that this will be her last year. She will be able to tell you just how you should go on, but don't let her, or that wild young brother of hers, lead you into mischief. She is a shocking harum-scarum. In fact her parents were obliged to send her to school because they could not keep a governess for more than a few weeks. Still, you can scarcely come to much harm in one afternoon, and I did not care to decline his lordship's invitation when it was so kindly worded.

He actually said that he had a great value for your Papa and that it was only right that their daughters should be friends. So no hiding yourself away in a corner. Join in whatever amusements are suggested, not putting yourself forward in any way but remembering that, on your mother's side, you are just as well connected as Lady Emma. Don't let her patronise you. She's the kind of girl you have to stand up to."

Katherine was naturally of a retiring disposition. Common sense told her that any attempt by a twelve-year-old newcomer to 'stand up to' one of the older girls would be very ill-received, even if it occurred on neutral ground, and the two were respectively hostess and guest. Desperately she wished that Aunt Julia was to accompany her, but the Earl had said that he would send the carriage for the "young lady and her abigail." At the time it had made her feel quite grown up to be going visiting on her own. It was only now that the full horror of her situation was borne in upon her. She would even be required to make conversation with the Countess, not, as usually happened, just to stand by Aunt Julia's side occasionally murmuring, "Yes," or "No," or "Thank you, ma'am," to such remarks as were addressed to her.

She revolved meekly for Aunt Julia's inspection. That lady approved the delicately embroidered ruffled lawn that Katherine was wearing, but sent her back to change her slippers; assured herself that she had her gloves and a clean handkerchief, and readjusted her sash. One of the maids came in, all excitement, to say that the carriage had arrived. Katherine quailed. She thought that her heart must have sunk right down into the pretty new slippers. She set her lips firmly to control their trembling, and climbed into the vehicle with all the enthusiasm of one bound for the stake.

It could, she supposed afterwards, have been worse. At least the Earl himself was not present. The Countess and Lady Emma received her, and after one or two tepid commonplaces about her growth and her forthcoming debut into the new world of school, the elder lady nodded permission when her daughter suggested that she and Katherine should repair to the stables, where Thomas would show the visitor round. The Countess considered that she had done all that hospitality required of her.

Katherine emerged into the open air with a sense of relief, and even contrived to utter one or two polite remarks about the beauty of the gardens through which they wended their way. She would have much preferred to remain on this comparatively safe and familiar ground. She was nervous of horses. Until these last few months, when Papa had decided that it was time for her to take her place in a wider world, she had lived in Town with him, cared for by a series of housekeepers and governesses who had done their conscientious best to fill the place of the child's long dead Mama. It had been a very quiet, secluded existence. Papa had kept carriage horses, of course, but it had never occurred to him to have his daughter taught to ride. The governesses tended to be middle-aged females of sedentary habit, grateful for the comfort of a well-sprung carriage when they wished to take the air, but not in the least addicted to equestrian exercise. If they had lived in the country, the subject of riding lessons for Katherine might have cropped up easily enough. In Town it simply did not arise.

When she was handed over to Mama's Cousin Julia to 'be made into a lady'—Papa's blunt phrase—her inadequacy in horsemanship had been discovered, but the matter was not one that could be remedied in a sennight. Lady Somersby was a brisk, sensible creature. She liked Katherine—though she wished the child showed more spirit—and she was sincerely grateful for the generous provision that John Martenhays had made for his daughter's maintenance while she was being initiated into the ways of her mother's world. It meant that Lady Somersby, a widow of straitened means, could once more afford one or two desirable luxuries. But to be setting up her own carriage or buying a pony for Katherine to ride would be foolish. The child would soon be going to school. She could take riding lessons there. Her Papa would willingly foot the bill for any extras that Lady Julia decreed were necessary for the education of a lady. Perhaps next summer a pony of her own might be considered. Lady Julia, accustomed to the exercise of rigid economy, thought of the expense of winter keep, and decided that next summer would be quite soon enough.

So Katherine approached the stables in considerable apprehension, though this she did her best to conceal, since Lady Emma seemed to think that she was giving her a high treat. When, however, it was put to her that she should borrow Lady Emma's outgrown habit and ride down to the village with the other two, she could not disguise her consternation.

"But I couldn't possibly," she gasped. "I'm very sorry, but I can't ride."

"Can't ride? A great girl of twelve and can't ride!" growled Lord Thomas in deep disgust. "Then what are we to do all afternoon. We were engaged to meet a friend in the village until your society was thrust upon us, and now you won't even bear us company. The last afternoon of the holidays, and a wretched brat that can't even ride to spoil all our fun." He lapsed into a sullen silence until an idea for alternative amusement suddenly struck him. "I'll tell you what," he exclaimed, with a grin of anticipation, "you get into Emma's habit and I'll teach you to ride."

Sheer terror at such an appalling prospect sharpened Katherine's wits. Somehow she kept her voice steady as she said, "Why don't you go and visit your friends as you had planned? I would be quite happy strolling about the grounds by myself. I don't wish to spoil your afternoon." Instinct warned her not to betray the dread that filled her at his proposal. He was just the kind of boy who would take a delight in teasing and frightening her, under the pretence of teaching her to ride.

But Emma shook her head. "That won't fit," she objected. "Mama might chance to see you and she would be sure to ask why you were alone."

"Then couldn't I wait here, in the stables? I could hide in one of the empty stalls if I heard anyone coming," pleaded Katherine. Anything would be better than the suggested riding lesson.

The other two consulted wordlessly and presently nodded. They could see only one flaw in the plan. "And you won't peach on us to Mama?" demanded Thomas.

Katherine looked puzzled.

"He means tell tales," elaborated his sister. "You won't tell her that we left you on your own. You'd better not. If you do, I'll see you well paid for it when we get to school."

Katherine drew herself up. "I don't know

much about school," she said steadily, "but I do know that one mustn't tell tales. I promise."

The stable seemed very quiet after the other two had gone. Emma had actually persuaded her brother to bring in a low bench from the harness room, considerate for once in her pleasure at the prospect of the afternoon's outing. It was not very clean, but it was better than nothing. Katherine seated herself carefully, gathering her dainty skirts so as to avoid sundry oil stains on the rough wood, and considered her position with a crooked little smile for the memory of Aunt Julia's injunction to join in whatever activity was suggested, and not to be hiding herself in a corner. Some two hours of solitude lay ahead of her. The stable clock, obligingly chiming the quarters, marked the slow passage of time. There was nothing to do and nothing of interest to see, and the only prospect of activity lay in the need to conceal herself if she heard any one approaching. But at least there was nothing to alarm her. The stalls in this part of the stable were all empty, Emma and Thomas having taken the last two horses.

Across the yard there were loose boxes, and through the dusty window she could occasionally see horses' heads protruding from the half doors. But they were safely shut in. In any case, she told herself determinedly, she was not really afraid of horses. It was just that she was not used to them; and they were big and strong and

a bit unpredictable. Even their head-tossing
was startling when you were not expecting it.
She got up and went to peer into the empty
stalls. There was not much to see except the hay
racks, scarcely visible in the gloom. It was not
even a very nice stable, she thought. The smell
was very strong, it was ill-lit, and there were
a great many flies. She went back to her bench
and gave herself up to rather miserable contem-
plation of her future. School loomed frighten-
ingly on the horizon. She hoped that few of her
schoolmates would resemble Lady Emma, and
was humbly thankful that she had not alienated
that intimidating young woman. It was all very
well for Aunt Julia to bid her hold her own.
Aunt Julia just didn't understand.

The stable clock struck three. She sighed.
Another hour at least; and on the thought came
the sound of approaching hoof-beats. Hurriedly,
she concealed herself in the nearest stall. There
was nothing to hide behind. She could only re-
treat to the farthest, darkest corner, hoping that
the newcomer was bound for one of the loose
boxes at the other side of the yard.

He was not. She heard the hooves come
nearer and nearer and stop. There was the mur-
mur of a pleasant young masculine voice, as the
rider dismounted and made much of his horse.
It was certainly not Thomas's voice. Next came
the slow approach of the led horse in the stable

entry. She held her breath, trying to estimate which stall he was making for.

It was sheer chance that she had chosen to hide in the stall where Dermot Winfield usually stabled Nelly. As an unconsidered poor relation, and a mere stripling at that, the servants in that ill-run household paid him little heed. The grooms were only too willing to let him tend his own mare, even though they grudgingly admitted that the animal was a nice bit o' blood. His comings and goings were not a signal for any unwonted display of activity in the stable, and he expected this one to be like all the rest, until Nelly took exception to the strange pale shape that crouched at the end of her stall, and stopped dead, her front feet braced against his onward impetus while she snorted her alarm and disapproval. His first thought was to soothe the mare, and only when she stopped shivering and sidling did he pay any heed to the intruder; to notice that she looked quite as distressed as Nelly.

He was a kindly lad, and his own circumstances had bred in him a sympathy for the weak and oppressed. It did not greatly surprise him to find a claimant on his pity lurking in his cousins' establishment. He knew his cousins.

"I'm so very sorry," he said pleasantly. "Did Nelly and I startle you? She will not hurt you, you know. She is the gentlest creature; follows my mother about like a pet dog. But of course

Mama has known her ever since she was foaled, and helped nurse her when she was sick. Horses are just like babies. The more you have to do for them the fonder you grow of them. Mama and Nelly love each other dearly. Being parted is a sad grief to them."

He talked on in this strain for a minute or two more, and his seventeen-year-old ability to chatter harmless commonplaces was becoming dangerously stretched before he saw a trace of colour return to the child's cheeks, and her bearing begin to relax from its taut composure. At last he ventured to say, "I presume that you are here to visit my cousins. Will you not permit me to escort you up to the house? You cannot wish to be loitering here in this dusty place. See, you have soiled your pretty dress already."

The mishap to her dress did not seem to distress the child, but the suggestion that she should go up to the house was a different matter. She clasped her hands together in an agitated way and said that she had promised his cousins to await their return in the stable.

"Then at least I can bear you company," returned Dermot cheerfully. "But I must unsaddle Nelly first, and rub her down, or she will think herself neglected."

He proceeded to attend to the mare. Katherine watched curiously, her shyness forgotten as the animal turned obediently under the ministering hands. Presently she even ventured a remark of her own. "She is very fond of you, isn't she?"

Dermot laughed and pushed aside the soft muzzle that was questing hopefully for the tit-bits that Nelly considered were her due.

"Cupboard love," he grinned. "Would you like to give her an apple? I have one in my pocket, as well she knows."

Greatly daring, Katherine thought that she would, and was shown how to hold the slices flat on her palm. Nelly took them daintily like the lady she was, and Katherine was encouraged to stroke the gleaming neck and to answer quite frankly and unashamedly when Dermot enquired about her own riding prowess. He was pleased to approve the information that she was to start lessons soon, explaining that an early start was essential to the development of real competence, and stressing the necessity of establishing good relations with one's mount by judicious fondling, and a good deal of soft-voice crooning talk. Katherine began to think that learning to ride might not, after all, be such a dreadful ordeal, and her questions came freely. Aunt Julia would have been surprised to see her timid little niece so much at ease with a strange young man. She did not even flinch when Nelly nudged her playfully, seeking more largesse, and only regretted that there was no more apple to give her.

The sound of the stable clock striking four

brought this pleasant little interlude to an end. Uneasiness showed itself again in Katherine's rather pale little face. The fondling hand grew still. Presently she crossed to the stable window and peered out. There was no sign of the young Dorseys. She turned to Dermot in some uncertainty.

"They said they would be back by four o'clock," she said slowly. "The carriage is to take me up at the half after and we were to have some refreshment first. If we don't go back to the house soon, I'm afraid some one will set out to look for us, and then it will all come out. Not that I would mind that, but I did promise not to tell— and they are sure to blame me."

Dermot looked at her compassionately. He had a pretty fair notion of the means that had been used to win her consent to remaining in the stable, all alone, for a whole afternoon, while the heedless pair were off about their own concerns. In any case that remark about 'not telling' and 'blame' was a dead give away.

"I take it that it was my aunt who was not to be told," he probed gently.

Katherine nodded.

"Then it is perfectly safe to go back to the house," he told her. "My aunt has driven out. Visiting, I must suppose. The carriage passed me in the avenue as Nelly and I were returning. The best thing you can do, if you wish to avoid notice, is to write a note for my cousins saying that as the time was so far advanced you have gone back to the house with me. No one will think it in the least strange, I promise you; and if Emma and Thomas have gone down to the village they may well have forgotten all about the time—and you—and might not be home till dusk. You can leave the note on that stool. They are bound to find it there."

Katherine hesitated briefly. It was difficult to accept that her new acquaintances could be so careless and forgetful, even when their own comfort was at stake. The knowledge that she would not have to face the formidable Countess, who might have asked questions that she could not answer, tipped the scales. Presumably the promised refreshment would be dispensed by the housekeeper, who was unlikely to ask any questions at all, especially if she, Katherine, returned to the house with a member of the family. She nodded agreement to Dermot's suggestion and accepted the offer of a leaf from his pocket book and the stump of a pencil for the writing of her note.

TWO

"You do me too much honour, milord," said Katherine punctiliously. "Pray do not think me the less appreciative that I feel myself obliged to decline your very obliging offer. Your friendship I must always value, but our tastes and our dispositions differ so widely that as life partners I feel that we should never suit."

This elegantly phrased set-down quite failed to abash Viscount Sandiford. "Oh, come, Kate," he told her cheerfully. "You can't treat me like that. Why! I've been counting on you this age past. You can't just reject me out of hand. It's not to assuage your pride, is it, because I paid some attention to the Melling chit last night? A pretty little creature, but she has not one

tenth of your wit and charm. It was just that
she seemed a little lonely, and I took pity on
her."

"Most commendable, I am sure," returned
Katherine drily. "It is a pity that she has not
one tenth of my expectations either. We might
then have been spared this rather mawkish
scene."

Lord Sandiford chuckled richly. "That is what
I like best about you, Kate. You deal as straight
as a man. What an excellent swordsman you
would have made if only the pastime were per-
missible to your sex."

"Meanwhile I must make do as best I can with
my wits and my tongue," retorted Katherine,
tartly, "and do not think to flummery me with
yours. We have dealt extremely together, largely
because you can always make me laugh—not
only at you, but at myself. A priceless asset. As
I said, your friendship I shall always value. But
if you imagine that this partiality blinds me to
your dealings with the muslin company, to your
hopeless addiction to gaming, or to the fact that
your pockets are wholly to let and your estates
grossly encumbered, permit me to inform you
that it does not. I am not innocent little Miss
Melling, Julian. Despite my claims to gentility,
I was bred up in business circles. I am twenty-
two years old and wide awake to the time of
day. I believe that you have a liking for me, and
to that belief you owe the degree of patience

that I have shown you. But that liking would not have prompted you to propose marriage if it were not for the money bags. It is not the first time that I have met this situation. Probably it will not be the last. But the answer is still and always, no. Somewhere in the world there may exist a man who would take me without my father's money. Till then; thank you, but no, thank you."

"Well, that is plain speaking indeed," said Viscount Sandiford, still quite unruffled. "But in common fairness, my dear Kate, have you ever considered the other side of the picture?"

One could not but like his good-tempered way of accepting a sharp snub, thought Katherine. If, indeed, he had accepted it.

"I am not your dear Kate," she countered, "but you may show me the other side of the picture if you feel that it will help me to a more just appreciation of my fellows."

"Never mind the other fellows," said his lordship bluntly. "Take one like me."

Katherine was too kind-hearted to retort that she had no intention of doing so. In any case, her companion was already in full flood of eloquence.

"Only son. Brought up to believe that it was my duty to marry. Eventually," he put in, hedging slightly as he saw Katherine's amused expression, and remembered that he was already eight and twenty. "Very old family—

succession to consider—that sort of thing. But a wife is an expensive item. Couldn't expect the poor girl to moulder away down at Sandiford all the time. Place is practically falling down. All right for a few weeks in the hunting season, but pretty Spartan even then for a gently bred girl. And one wouldn't marry any other sort."

For a moment it seemed as though the blood of that long line of proud ancestors stiffened his indolent pose, and Katherine treasured an unconscious compliment. Mongrel bred she might be—according to her father—but this suitor, at least, did not share that opinion.

"That means we spend a good part of the year in Town," continued the earnest orator. "My bachelor apartment is very snug, but not big enough for two, so I must hire a house and servants to run it. Even if we content ourselves with a female cook instead of a proper chef, we must have a butler and a kitchen boy, and at least half a dozen female servants. All this apart from the expense of setting up a small stable. Nothing ostentatious, naturally, but I couldn't have m'wife driving hireling commoners. Then there would be her dress bills to be paid. My mother always paid hers, I know. Only time she and my father really quarrelled. Stuck to it that Madame wouldn't oblige her with any more gowns until the bill was paid. So what with one thing and another you can see that it would soon run into several thousands—and that's without the cost of entertaining. Do you wonder that a fellow looks about him for a partner that's pretty well inlaid? Can't expect him to stand that sort of nonsense without a bit of support, can you now?"

Katherine compressed her lips firmly to conceal a strong inclination to smile at this ingenious bit of special pleading. It would be a mistake to show any trace of sympathy with his predicament; would only encourage him in the belief that she might change her mind. She said primly, "I can see that you have been giving a good deal of thought to the question of marriage. If, as you say, you believe it to be your duty to marry, such consideration is very necessary. But your attitude confirms me in the belief that I am not the right partner for you. I would certainly expect any prospective husband to be in a position to support me in modest comfort. If he had not the means to do so, then he would be obliged to master his natural impatience to make me his bride until he had made shift to remedy the deficiency."

"What! Even though you had more than enough for the pair of you?" exclaimed Lord Sandiford in genuine amazement.

"Perhaps the more so for that reason," returned Katherine firmly. And as he made no attempt to conceal his puzzlement, she went on quietly, "I am not of your order, milord. In the circles in which you are accustomed to moving

I am well aware that such marriages as you describe are commonplace and perfectly acceptable. Generally speaking, one party contributes the wealth, the other brings rank or an ancient name. All I am saying is that it is not the kind of marriage for me. You must remember that I grew up in a different world. My father was the third son of a country squire of modest means. He was given a good education and left to make his own way in the world. You know how well he used his talents and his opoortunities. That is why you are here with me today. But I, if ever I marry, will choose a man of my father's stamp. His fortune may be modest enough, but like my father he will work and study to improve it. Nor will he despise the honest toil that forwards his prosperity. Such a man would consider it his right to support his wife. If she chanced to be well-dowered he might even prefer that her money should be tied up in trust for her children."

That was going a bit too far, she thought. She was making this mythical suitor sound positively priggish. But Julian's nonchalant good humour was quite equal to the situation. He was prepared to discuss the case with genuine interest.

"Shouldn't think so for a moment," he objected. "Not that fusty sort of fellow. Wouldn't want his children coming into the world all hosed and shod. He'd want 'em to learn to stand

on their own feet, and not be depending on inherited trust funds. Besides, he'd want to set
the money to work to make more. You'd do far
better to settle for an easy-going fellow like me,
and so I shall still hope to persuade you. But no
use trying to do so while you are all taken up
with this paragon of all the hard working vir-
tues. Who is he? Do I know him?"

"For all I know you may well do so," Katherine told him. And then, at his startled expression, she relented and added, "I certainly don't.
He's just an idea. I haven't even imagined what
he might look like. And since you seem to understand his reactions to trust funds and idle
wealth, you seem to know him just as well as
I do. Why don't you take a leaf out of his book?
You've brains enough if you would only apply
them. You might even achieve the relief of your
financial necessities by a simpler means than
marriage."

"But my good Kate! So much virtue! I should
die of boredom before the year was out. Or I
should be driven to such excesses by way of relief, as would quite set society by the ears.
Which reminds me that I am appointed to drive
Lady Snattisham in the Park this morning, and
if I don't wish to set her at outs with me, I had
best bid you farewell. Don't dream too long over
your paragon; I promise you he would be a dead
bore and most unamusing as a husband."

Julian certainly had the knack of getting over

awkward ground lightly, reflected Katherine, when he had made his airy farewells. There was certainly no suggestion of the rejected suitor about his jaunty bearing as he ran lightly down the front steps.

Lady Julia came in quietly. "You rejected him, I suppose? Not that it would have been a good match for you. His social position is everything that is to be desired, but he is all to pieces, of course. And, while he has an engaging personality, his morals leave a good deal to be desired. You were right to refuse him. But the thing is, my dear, that you have refused so many offers, and two of them really brilliant ones. Your situation is difficult, I allow. No girl wishes to be sought for her expectations alone. But I do not believe that such gentlemen as Mr. Beldon or Sir Robert Pendridge would have paid their addresses if your appearance and personality were not pleasing. Perhaps I am being foolish beyond permission, but it seems to me that even now you have still not outgrown your childish diffidence. Do you remember how I was for ever urging you to set a higher value on yourself? Yet here you are, twenty two years old, nearing the end of your third highly successful season, and you still cannot bring yourself to believe in the sincerity of your friends and admirers."

"I might have believed in it more easily if I had not suffered one or two disillusioning experiences in my early teens. Because I was a quiet, docile child, a good many adults seemed to think that I was stupid, too. Once I actually heard the mother of one of my school friends describing Papa's circumstances to an acquaintance, while I was standing plainly in her sight—and wondering how best I could creep tactfully away. She said that she had encouraged Hildegarde to invite me home for the holidays because one never knew when a man of such wealth and influence might not prove useful. I liked Hildegarde; I still do, but I don't think I ever felt quite the same towards her afterwards. None of the other incidents were quite so blatant, but an impression once made"— and if she had spoken truth she would have admitted that it dated back to that unfortunate visit to the Priory before she had even gone to school—"reinforced by a hint here and there, and it is difficult to believe that any one is disinterested."

In a sudden access of feeling she turned sharply on her chaperone. "Even you, my love. Be honest, now. I know that you love me dearly, as indeed I love you, who have been the nearest to a mother that I have ever known. But can you be disinterested? Does not your comfort rest to some extent on the allowance that Papa pays you while I am in your charge? Both you and he express your pleasure in my modest social success, but do you never wonder what will become of you if I choose to accept one of these gentlemen who honour me by requesting my hand in marriage?"

She dropped on her knees and buried her face in her chaperone's lap. "Oh, dear Aunt Julia! Don't you see how the money distorts everything? Even your kindness."

"Of course I do. And you are perfectly right. I have often wondered what would become of me when you were no longer in my charge, because, you know, one so soon becomes accustomed to the standard of comfort that your father's generosity has provided. But at least you can rely upon your Papa. Undoubtedly he will make provision for me—probably an annuity—so you have no need to fear any partiality on my part if I commend one of your suitors too highly or seem to disparage another. Poor child." She smoothed the bowed head. "What I can see is that you are quite worn out with all the excitements of the season, and sorely in need of a period of rest and relaxation. Will you not change your mind and come with me, after all, to Brighton? The sea air must have an invigorating effect, and I do not mean to be very gay. A few concerts and assemblies, perhaps, but, to be honest, I am more interested in the libraries and the coffee drinkings and, of course, the shops."

Katherine pulled herself out of her temporary abandonment. "Dear Aunt Julia," she said affectionately. "You should rather be berating me for ill-humour and intemperate speech, than uttering soothing noises. But at least I will not burden you with my presence in Brighton. You shall enjoy a well deserved rest. I will go down to Hays Park to Papa, as we arranged."

"And your future plans?" reminded Lady Julia gently.

Katherine moved restlessly. "I do not know. I feel I cannot endure another Season, just frittering my life away in following the social round. I know that it pleases Papa, but he has no notion how boring it is, nor how hollow is the success that he rates so high. Perhaps I may have more chance to talk with him, now that he has largely withdrawn from his business interests; perhaps, even to convince him of the futility of my present way of life. For surely the chief object of making one's debut and following the dreary routine is to catch a husband. And I do not think that I shall every marry."

Lady Julia flung up her hands in horror. "My dear child! You cannot be serious. What else is there for a woman to do? You can only spend so much of your time in good works. You have already enjoyed every cultural opportunity that one can readily call to mind, and you cannot indulge in extensive travel since conditions on the continent forbid. If you do not marry—and even an arranged marriage would be better than none, since you would at least have the comfort of your children—you will dwindle into a religious minded spinster, whose only interest lies in deciding whether or no the Vicar has a tendency towards Rome. When your father dies—and it is in the nature of things that he will pre-decease you—you will have the added occupation of changing your will as the whim moves you. Surely even the Season, with the possibility that you may yet find a husband to your fastidious liking, is better than that?"

"Much better," agreed Katherine, laughing rather wryly at the picture that her aunt had conjured up. "Almost you persuade me to recall Lord Sandiford."

"And I daresay you could beckon him back by lifting an eyebrow," nodded Lady Julia. "But you'll do better than Sandiford. Poor boy." She expended a brief sigh, tribute to his lordship's easy charm.

"Aunt Julia, what does become of all the debutantes who don't marry?" said Katherine suddenly. "I suppose most of them have families who will support them in a fashion. They will be spinster aunts to their more fortunate sisters' children. Useful and put upon, their comfort little considered. But how about girls like Camilla Westwell? She is perfectly beautiful, you will agree, of high pedigree and quite charming. But worse than penniless, because she has three sisters treading on her heels. What will become of her if she does not receive a respectable offer?

For I am a little acquainted with her, and I fear that she has not received one yet."

"Her Mama is too eager, and does the girl disservice thereby," said Lady Julia, reluctantly. "It is very sad. Every one knows the state of Westwell's affairs, and four daughters is a cross for any family to bear, especially as the estate is entailed and will go to a cousin. Left to herself the child might well have achieved a modest match. She is, as you say, quite charming. But Mama was maladroit, following up the smallest sign of interest with an eagerness too great; which only served to frighten possible suitors away."

"Whereas if the poor little wretch had been possessed of even a modest dowry, she might by now be comfortably established," pointed out Katherine a little wearily. "Do you wonder that I detect interested motives in most of my suitors, and doubt the efficacy of my very moderate charms?"

Lady Julia tried to persuade her that the cases were quite different, but none of her arguments succeeded in raising Katherine's spirits. She finally abandoned them in favour of a suggestion that they should drive to the circulating library and exchange their books. Katherine, falling in with this innocuous proposal, went off to change into a carriage dress.

THREE

Katherine arrived at Hays Park at the end of June. Her father, who spent most of his time in his country home, now that he had largely turned over his city interests to his associates, greeted her with affection and promptly took her to task for not going to Brighton with her aunt.

"Nothing for you to do here, child," he complained, "and well I know that it is only a sense of duty that brings you. I suppose you think I must be lonely or bored, living here in the country, and may take to fancying myself neglected; but I promise you that it's no such thing. It's a fascinating business, this agriculture, if you could only persuade some of its devotees that it is a business, like any other, and will show a fair profit if you practise the right methods. Will they listen? Not a jot. Everything must be done exactly as it was in their father's day, or even in their grandfather's. All the miracles of modern invention at their service—and do they make use of 'em? They speak of seed drills and four-coulter ploughs as though they were inventions of the Devil; and enclosing waste land or combining two or three small holdings into one larger one that can be run more economically is a black sin. The only point on which we see eye to eye is selective stock breeding. They can see the point of that, and most of them have a good eye for a beast. But what between insisting that my own men use the machines that I've bought, and trying to make some of my neighbours see sense, I've no time to mope."

Katherine managed to convince him that inclination rather than duty had brought her home.

"The peace of the countryside is very refreshing after the dust and noise of London. I had no desire at all to go to Brighton, which will be just as noisy if less dusty. Besides, I wanted to consult with you—when you are less preoccupied with your new hobby."

Her father declared himself all attention, adding that one of the delights of country life was that most of the work could be done at a leisurely pace. "I meant to take a stroll down to the ten-acre to see how the wheat is coming on. They tell me it's never grown wheat before, but I reckon that after the cultivation it's had I'll get a fair crop. Come with me if you're not too tired, and we can talk as we go."

It seemed to Katherine that her father's absorption in his new way of life would add force to her own argument. A little awkwardly at first, for she did not wish to appear ungrateful, gaining confidence as he listened patiently to her rather faltering explanation, she spoke of her growing disenchantment with the life of the frivolous society damsel.

"Pray do not think I have been unhappy, Papa. Indeed, during the first Season I liked it very well. But the next one, and now this last one offered little variety. The same people at the same parties; the same drives in the Park or strolls through the Botanical Gardens. The Opera, the Assemblies, the Play. You will be thinking that I am above being pleased, for I had lovely clothes and the kindest of chaperones—everything that a reasonable girl could desire. And truly I am grateful for your care of me, and for your generosity. Aunt Julia explained to me that you wanted me to have all the advantages that my Mama enjoyed in her youth, and to lead the kind of life that she lead before her marriage. I think that I have done so, but I am sorry, Papa it is not enough. Perhaps I am too much your daughter. You spoke just now of people who wanted to do everything exactly as it had always been done, never making any changes, never learning anything new. And to me Society is like that. Not that I am a rebel against convention. Most of it is good and sensible, meant for one's comfort and safety. But why should we despise people who do things—like inventing the machines that you spoke of? Why should I gloss over the fact that you are my Papa, and always speak rather of Mama's genteel relations? I am proud of what you have achieved. I only wish that it was possible for a female to make a useful and successful life for herself. That is what I would like to so. Something useful, however small. Something that would help people. But it is difficult when you are a girl and not particularly clever; I don't even have any talent that I could develop. I don't sing or paint, and my devotion to good works is, I'm ashamed to say, only tepid. It has always been easier to give money—your money—for the relief of necessity, rather than to become personally involved. What am I to do, Papa? When I hear others speak of all that is going on in the world today, I feel that there must be a place where I could help. But where?"

John Martenhays did not immediately rush into facile comfort. The sincerity of the appeal had touched him deeply. He felt closer to this daughter of his than he had ever done, and he understood that much as she resembled her

Mama in physical appearance—the frail, slender build; the small pale face, and the big dark eyes, yet there was in her a tough, questing spirit inherited from himself. Perhaps he had done wrong to shelter and cosset her as he had tried to do. Yet, as she herself had said, what could one do with a girl? There could have been no place for her in his workaday life. It had seemed natural enough to turn to his wife's cousin and arrange for her to supply the motherly care and the social background that the girl needed. So she had been given her schooling at a highly select academy and had taken her place in her mother's world. It was what his wife would have wished, and by all accounts she had made a success of it. He was glad of that. It added enormously to the value of what she had just said. She was not a failure, rejecting a world that had defeated her. She had simply decided that she wanted more from life than the social round could offer. He felt the same. But he, luckily, was a man.

Presently he said temperately, "I believe that many women find the deepest satisfaction in marriage. Making a home for a husband and children might well fulfil your desire to be of use. Naturally I am aware that you have received a number of offers of marriage. Most of the gentlemen paid me the courtesy of asking my permission to address you. Have you not found, among their number, one whom you would choose as a husband?"

"No, Papa." And then, since the mood seemed right for open confession, "Nor one whom I could not feel was influenced more by my expectations than by his need of me."

Her father nodded slowly. "I know. But don't despair. It was not my money that prompted your Mama to accept my hand in marriage. It seems an odd thing to be saying to one's daughter, but we truly loved one another. I met her in the most difficult circumstances. Her father was trying to raise a large loan, practically unsecured, and I had been instructed to refuse it. Which I did. Then she came in with a tray of wine and cakes; meant to sweeten me up, we always joked one another. They had only the one servant, and she had just stepped out on an errand. Your grandfather could do no less than introduce us, wanting my good will as he did, and that began it. But I was only a junior partner then, with all my way to make, so it was not the prospect of wealth that steeled her to resist all the pressure that was put upon her to send me about my business. Poverty poor as they were, her folk couldn't reconcile themselves to her marrying into trade, though my bank could have bought them up ten times over and never noticed it. We won through in the end, she and I, and had three years of such happiness as I'll never forget. That's why I say don't despair. It's worth waiting for. And you'll know soon enough that it's you and not the money. If you're my daughter, as you say, you'd soon detect a sham."

Katherine laughed. "It concerns me more to be able to recognise an honest man when I meet one," she said ruefully. "I fear that my disposition is suspicious rather than gullible. It may be a safeguard, but it adds a bitter tang to all one's pleasure. Sometimes I wish that I could trust more readily."

Her father nodded thoughtfully. "Best not," he told her. "When you're tempted to trust, wait. Make sure. Trust, too freely given, is a sore hurt when it is betrayed. Be on good terms with people by all means. You don't have to trust them till time brings confidence."

They had reached the wheat-field, and talk turned to impersonal matters as Mr. Martenhays studied the growing crop, appraising the upstanding straw, estimating the possible yield and outlining the kind of weather that he would indent for when it came to harvest time, if only the Almighty would take account of his needs. They did not revert to the former topic until they met again over the dinner table.

Since there were only the two of them, they dined informally, Katherine ending her meal with a succulent peach from the succession houses, while her father sipped his wine.

"This is very comfortable," he said presently.

"And don't think I'm not very well pleased to have you at home again. But I'm afraid it will be very dull for you. I'm not much of a one for socialising, myself, and not being a hunting man I haven't mixed over much with my neighbours. In fact," he looked a little ashamed, "there's been a bit of falling out amongst us. Nothing serious." He hastened to allay any alarm that she might feel. "Just that argument gets a bit heated from time to time. I never was one to hide my teeth and maybe I've been a bit too outspoken, and me only a Johnny Newcome. But I never could abide stupidity. And then, too, I doubt I've been too successful. Most of my innovations have worked pretty well. If I'd made a few mistakes—made a fool of myself now and then, as no doubt I will, given time enough—I'd be more popular. Only, meanwhile, it's a bit hard on you. I daresay some of the neighbours will call, once they hear that you're back home, but there's not so many young folk, and you'll soon get tired of spending all your days listening to a lot of old fogies."

"Older people usually have something interesting to talk about," said Katherine quietly. "Some of the younger ones are only interested in themselves. But we shall see. For the present I mean to be idle. If the weather is kind, I shall revisit some of the haunts of my childhood. Do you realise that it is nearly ten years since I spent a long holiday at home? I shall walk with you about the fields if you will have me, and ride every day. And I am planning an orgy of reading and needlework for the wet days. You need not think that I intend to cut up all your peace by demanding parties and entertainments to keep me amused. And since you have just confessed that you are not one for socialising, you cannot scold me if I, too, prefer to live quietly."

Mr. Martenhays protested that the cases were very different, but she would have none of it. A quiet country holiday was just what she wanted at the moment. Time to make plans for the future. Mr. Martenhays was very dubious, but he held his peace.

Katherine put her programme into effect from the very next day. She found the strolling walks in her father's society, the gentle, leisurely rides, and the evenings devoted to books and sewing, and an occasional idle tinkering with the pianoforte entirely to her present taste. Insensibly she relaxed, now that she was no longer in the public eye. Her laughter came easily. Even a small joke seemed funny when shared with Papa. She settled comfortably into the slow-paced days. As Papa had predicted, some of the neighbours called. She found them, on the whole, friendly and pleasant. No one seemed to have any particular axe to grind, not even the Vicar when he spoke of the cost of repairing the roof of the nave. He obviously trusted that the Lord, assisted by his parishioners, would eventually provide. It might have seemed unfortunate that most of the visitors were middle aged, and that their families were a little younger than Katherine, but at the present stage of her affairs it did not disappoint her. She felt the need for solitude rather than the society of her compeers.

It was in this peaceful, relaxed mood that she turned her horse's head towards the Priory, one morning, when she had been at home about a month. She smiled a little for the memories of that long ago visit to the Dorsey home. Even the mare she was riding was a reminder. She had called her Nelly after Dermot Winfield's mount, the first animal that she had ever ventured to fondle. She had not forgotten Mr. Winfield, either, though she had never met him again. Emma Dorsey had mentioned him once or twice, rather contemptuously, as a poor relation who spent his holidays with them because his parents were abroad. Then Emma had left school, and the brief contact was broken. But ten years had brought vast changes to the Priory. Scraps of information had reached Katherine's ears from time to time after she had been launched into Society. There had been Emma's marriage, at the age of eighteen, to a wealthy merchant old enough to be her father. There had been the death of Lord Thomas from wounds received in a duel—a duel which, in one of his drunken, bullying moods, he had forced upon an inexperienced-seeming stripling. It was unfortunate for Thomas that the stripling chanced to be a skilled exponent of the small sword. Thomas's blustering style was quite outmatched, and it was only thanks to his opponent's generosity that he was not killed. A pity, then, that this generosity was brought to naught by Thomas's subsequent behaviour. Having lost a deal of blood, he proceeded to drink himself into a stupor. Recovering slightly, feverish and uncomfortable, he refused to have a surgeon tend his wounds. There was no one to make him yield to proper treatment, and he sought relief from his increasing pain in the brandy bottle. When his ramblings, half drunken, half delirious, frightened his man into sending for the doctor, it was already too late.

The old Earl had not long survived his son and heir. The Countess had gone to live with her married daughter, and it was generally understood that the estate would have to be sold up, so desperate was the state of the Earl's finances.

That had not happened. Somehow, the poor relation, Dermot Winfield, had bought up mortgages, sold timber and one or two outlying fields, and was eking out a hand to mouth existence in the bailiff's cottage. The Priory itself was reduced to a skeleton staff, most of them too old to seek employment elsewhere, kept on by their employer's humanity, but few of them capable of a full day's work. Every one said that young Winfield was mad to sink his modest inheritance in attempting to bring such a decayed place into proper shape. It was not even as though he stood to inherit the title, he being descended from the Dorseys on the distaff side, through his mother, Lady Frances Dorsey, who had married a military man, a mere commoner.

The mere commoner had known how to hold household. He had left his son in a position to safeguard his mother's comfort until her tragically early death, and also to launch out, however precariously, on the restoration of the Priory estate.

Katherine was seized by a sudden whim to re-visit the place. She had no desire to meet Mr. Winfield—doubted if she would even recognise him—but there might be a gardener or a caretaker of some kind, who would admit her to the grounds—perhaps even to the house itself. Such behaviour was commonplace when a house held any architectural or historic interest. A handsome tip to the servant who did the honours, and everything was made smooth. She assured herself that her purse was in the pocket of her habit, and rode down the lane to the main gate.

FOUR

"I remember you now, Hilda. Pray forgive me for not recognising you at once. You used to be one of the abigails at Hays Park when I was a little girl."

"That's it, Miss Katherine. 'Bout seven you would be when I left. Small wonder that you didn't remember me. I took a post as housekeeper to his late Lordship and the Countess, and thought I was bettering myself."

It was a flat statement. The listener was left to draw her own conclusions, until the housekeeper added another piece of information. "Mind, it was through coming to the Priory that I met Armstrong, so maybe it was all for the best, for he's a kind husband and a good worker.

Mrs. Armstrong I am now, and my husband used to be the estate carpenter. He still does all that has to be done in his own line, but nowadays we've all got to turn our hands to any job that needs doing. I'm sure I never thought to go back to polishing furniture, and even helping out in the kitchen at a pinch. But with so much to be done and so few of us to do it, not to mention the way Mr. Winfield is always there where the work's heaviest and hardest, you don't fancy standing on your rights and saying it's no part of your job."

Katherine was intrigued. She said politely, "It is very good of you to take time to show me about when you are so busy."

Her groom had found an ancient gardener who had assured them that it would be quite in order for them to see over the house and gardens—"such as they are"—and added that he would undertake to keep an eye on the horses. He had then handed them over to the housekeeper, who had turned out to be an old friend.

"I'm afraid there's little enough to see," she said now. "Everything in the principal rooms is under holland covers. The main staircase is thought to be very fine and the carvings that adorn the library fireplaces are much admired. But it is all sadly neglected, miss. Indeed I'm ashamed that you should see it as it is, and me responsible for it. If only I had half a dozen strong young girls, or even a sturdy footman or two. But the master says that the land must come first. All his prosperity depends on that. The house must wait its turn—and the roof leaking in fifty different places, according to which way the wind blows. Small wonder that the tapestries are mouldering away and the panelling grey with damp."

It seemed that having found a sympathetic audience in whom to confide, Mrs. Armstrong might continue in this strain indefinitely. As she led the way from room to room she pointed out to Katherine the various features that were generally considered worthy of interest, but punctuated her recital with sorrowful references to the ravages that occurred in houses that were too long shut up. Katherine could see for herself that dust lay thick on surfaces that should have gleamed with polish, but nothing could detract from the beautifully proportioned rooms or the magnificent staircase. There was singularly little furniture, but the exquisite plaster mouldings saved the room from looking too bare, even though in some places the plaster was discoloured by damp. Katherine thought she could have spent the whole morning in gazing at the oak panels in the hall and on the staircase itself, which featured a design of flowers, fruit and foliage, so natural, yet so delicate, that it was difficult to believe that it had been carved by human hands. Katherine had never

seen anything one half so fine, and her frank
admiration gratified her attendant's heart.

"If you likes carvings, miss, come and see the
over-mantel in the library," that lady invited.
"I don't know much about such matters myself,
but it was always greatly admired by the visitors that used to come about the house in the
old days. The Dutch school, they said it was."

The over-mantel was of carved marble and
very beautiful, but Katherine preferred the
warmth of the staircase to the cold perfection
of these classical deities and well nourished
cherubs. The library itself seemed more habitable than the other reception rooms, perhaps
because the book-filled shelves that lined the
walls gave it a lived-in look. But Mrs. Armstrong said that it was never used these days.
The master rarely set foot in the house itself
unless it was to inspect some new show of damp
or decay reported by one of the servants.

"Such as this," she continued gloomily, leading the way into a small saloon next to the library which Katherine recognised. It was here
that the Countess had received her on that
memorable first visit. She distinctly remembered the tapestry that almost covered one wall.
And it was this tapestry that her guide indicated. "Moth," she said tragically, and pointed
out to Katherine the damage that the grubs had
wrought. Katherine exclaimed sympatheti-

cally, suggesting that the hanging could probably be repaired by a skilled needlewoman.

"It's not as though it were silk," she said thoughtfully, "and I should think you could match the colours of that wool easily enough. It's only the surface that is damaged. The warp seems sound enough."

But Mrs. Armstrong only said gloomily that the one servant who had any claim to being a sewing maid was fully occupied with keeping clothing and household linen in decent repair. "Let alone that she's nearly seventy, and I doubt that her eyes are as good as they were. She'd never be able to set about a job like that. A pity, because the master had a fondness for that particular tapestry. Seems he used to study it when he was a little lad, and try to make out what all the monks were doing."

As well he might, thought Katherine. It was certainly an unusual bit of work. She did not think it was particularly valuable, but it was probably unique. It might possibly have been worked by some lady of the Priory of long ago, with the help of her maids. The background was recognisably the south front of the house itself, with the courtyard in front of it, and the foreground—and every other available corner—was devoted to representations of monks. There were monks digging in the garden; monks tending the sick; giving out food to the beggars at the gate. There were monks singing in the choir;

writing in the library; painting; giving out stores; supervising the preparation of food, in a kitchen with a cavernous hearth. No wonder that a small boy had found it as entertaining as a picture book, and had developed a fondness for it.

Katherine yielded to impulse. She did not know quite what moved her. Perhaps she was already wearying of her rather dawdling life; perhaps she wanted to repay a small kindness shown to her years ago. In any case the work itself appealed to her strongly. "I could mend it for you," she said slowly. "I would enjoy doing it. And if Mr. Winfield never comes into the house he need know nothing about it until it is finished. But I should have to work on it here."

Mrs. Armstrong protested at first but was easily won over once she was convinced that Katherine really would enjoy doing the work. The temptation to "have a bit of young life about the place" was a strong one, and she proved fertile in imagination, suggesting that Katherine should ride over in the mornings, as she had done today, work in the library while the light was good—and the master safely occupied out of doors—have a bite of luncheon with her old friend and ride back in the afternoon.

They considered this plan in detail and found no fault with it, Katherine saying that she would have to purchase suitable materials for the repair, as she had nothing appropriate in her workbox; and adding that she would not make the long ride if the weather was too unfavourable. She was then invited to partake of tea and cakes in the housekeeper's room before taking her departure.

Within a week, she had made a little niche for herself in the secluded, busy world of the Priory. Most of the servants knew of her presence, and would enquire politely as to the progress of her task if their duties brought them to the library. Mrs. Armstrong would bring her a cup of coffee or chocolate to refresh her after her ride, and would linger for a moment or two watching how deftly the needle replaced the damaged threads. It was slow work, but Katherine enjoyed it, and after some initial nervousness—for she was, after all, meddling with Mr. Winfield's property without his permission—her confidence grew steadily as the success of the attempt grew daily more apparent.

Sometimes, to ease the weariness of sitting still for long hours, she would stroll in the big bare rooms, or finger the books on the library shelves. She never encountered Mr. Winfield. There was something a little conspiratorial in the manner in which Mrs. Armstrong would casually inform her of his probable movements, so that she could avoid meeting him in her comings and goings. The main danger lay in the chance that he would visit the stables and enquire why two strange horses were standing

there, but Mrs. Armstrong did not take it very
seriously. It was unlikely in the first case, since
Mr. Winfield's days were so strictly planned
that only emergency would bring him to the
stables without warning; and if he did notice
the strange horses he would naturally assume
that someone had come to look over the house,
just as Katherine herself had done on that first
occasion. Though the Priory buildings themselves were a crumbling ruin, the house was of
some historic and architectural interest, and
such visitors were not unknown. The only suf-
ferer was Katherine's young groom, who was
obliged to spend his mornings in yawning boredom so severe that he eventually fell into the
way of performing a number of odd jobs about
the stables, much to the gratification of the ancient coachman, who still ruled the place as
though he had half a dozen grooms and any
number of stable hands to carry out his com-
mands. Young Jasper enjoyed the old man's
rambling tales of former glories, and respected
his undoubted knowledge of horseflesh; so the
pair got on surprisingly well together and Jasper's boredom was in part alleviated.

As the number of whole and hearty monks
depicted in the tapestry increased week by
week, Katherine discovered in herself a growing respect for the tapestry's owner. She could
not help finding out a good deal about him from
Hilda's reports of his daily activities. He seemed

to do the work of two men, and his versatility was amazing. She knew from her father how each trade within a farm was jealously preserved by its own artisans, but Mr. Winfield seemed to know sufficient about sheep and cattle, pasture and arable, and even fencing and draining to hold the respect and even the surly affection of his employees. Or was it his kindness to the number of elderly retainers, who must surely have been cast upon the Parish if he had not given them employment? Finding even small wages for so many who could do only light work must be a heavy drain on a man who was struggling to restore a neglected estate, and who could probably find five different ways to lay out every penny he possessed.

She ventured to express this opinion to Hilda, who entirely agreed. "Not even as though we had been his own servants," she pointed out. "Seems as though he inherited us along with neglected acres and mortgages. It's a sad pity those jewels were never found. Worth a fortune if all the tales were true."

"What jewels are those?" asked Katherine, threading her needle with a strand of crimson wool.

"Why, it's an old tale. Missing for fifty or sixty years, they've been. I doubt if anybody knows the rights of it now. The Earl of that day—Mr. Winfield's great grandfather he would be—held by the Stuart cause. Not openly, of course, but

he sent money to buy arms, and to support the
one he called his rightful Monarch. And when
Prince Charles Edward landed in Scotland in
'45, Mr. Winfield allowed his elder son to travel
north to join him. The younger boy was in
France, and him just new-wed. People reckoned
that he was up to his neck in plotting and rebellion, too, but so far as is known he never bore
arms in the campaign."

The narrative ran so smoothly that Katherine guessed it had been oft repeated. Even the
rather stilted language sounded strange on
Hilda's homely tongue. But the story was a new
view point on the chequered history of the
Priory. She settled herself comfortably to listen.

It was a tragic tale. The failure of the Jacobite
rebellion had ruined the Dorseys. The elder boy
had died at Culloden. His brother had fled to
France once more, and had eked out a poverty
stricken existence with his young wife, depen-
dent largely on the charity of friends.

"But you mentioned lost jewels. Where do
they come into the story?" demanded Katherine.

"They belonged to the old Earl—the one that
was accused of treasonable practices. They had
been his wife's, part of her dowry and worth a
mint. There was a diamond necklace alone that
would have bought an estate, and then there
were sapphires and other stones that were
worth a lot of money.

It seems the old man was given reason to suspect that he stood in danger of arrest; that his estates would be confiscated and he himself imprisoned, if not beheaded. No doubt he had friends in government circles who kept him well informed. Moreover, he was in poor health. He had already suffered one paralytic seizure and his doctors predicted that any shock might bring on another which could prove fatal. Whatever his reasons, he made a will leaving the jewels to his surviving son's wife. She came of a good Whig family, and there was no evidence against her husband. Perhaps the old man had the idea of saving something from the wreck of his fortunes. If his estates were confiscated, at least the jewels might be saved. In fact, he died before the government moved against him, and although his younger son succeeded to the title he remained abroad. His daughter, The Lady Frances, who became Mr. Winfield's mother, was born shortly after her grandfather's death.

When, two years later, her father died, there was no one to oppose the succession of a cousin who had always been loyal to the Hanoverian interest. But when the widowed Countess put in a claim for the jewels they were nowhere to be found. The house was searched time and time again but to no avail. Various theories were put forward. Some thought that the elder brother had taken the diamonds with him when he rode north to join the young prince; others that his brother had taken them to France and disposed of them there. The only solid fact emerging from all this speculation was that they were gone. It was fortunate for the Lady Frances that her mother's connections were comfortably placed and could afford to support her, and that she was married, in her first season, to a military gentleman of respectable fortune. But it did not alter the fact that the jewels were rightfully hers, and could have made all the difference to her son's situation if only they could be discovered.

"You say the house has been searched again and again?"

Hilda nodded. "In the early days, yes. I don't know that the family troubled themselves a great deal after that. The jewels weren't theirs you see. And neither Lady Frances nor her mother ever lived here, though Lady Frances paid one or two visits during the early years of her marriage. But nothing was ever found."

"I expect the jewels were sold for the furtherance of the Stuart cause," said Katherine. "If the old man was in poor health his mind might not have been perfectly clear. He might have forgotten that he had already disposed of them."

Hilda looked doubtful. "Myself, I wouldn't think you could forget a thing like that. Not when he showed sense enough to bequeath them to somebody who wasn't tainted with treason.

Sometimes I still hope they'll turn up. But meanwhile I'd better be about my proper work instead of gossiping here. I'll miss you sore when you go, and that's a fact. And it's nearly finished, isn't it?"

"Another day or two," nodded Katherine, leaning back to study the result of her labours. "And just as well. The days are drawing in. My father does not like me being abroad after dusk."

To speak truth, Mr. Martenhays had little enthusiasm for any aspect of his daughter's self-imposed task. He had not cared to forbid it, for he could not really see that she could come to any harm. The presence of Hilda Armstrong was a sop to the proprieties, and the Priory's new owner did not actually live on the premises. Nevertheless, the situation was sufficiently unusual to make him uneasy, and only his sympathy with his daughter's desire for useful occupation had persuaded him to countenance it. Unlike Hilda, he would be thankful when the task was completed.

Two days later this happy eventuality occurred. The last monk was busy about his task; the last thread was woven into the background. By ones and twos such servants as were about the house slipped in to view the completed tapestry, and to assure the needlewoman that it looked as good as new.

The remark, repeated for the third time,

moved Katherine to wonder just when the tapestry actually had been new. Pretty soon after
the dissolution of the monasteries, she suspected, when first the Priory had come into lay
ownership, and while the occupations that filled
the lives of the monastic orders were still familiar to everyone. She wondered if there was
any reference to it in the voluminous histories
of the family that filled a whole section of the
library shelves. Once or twice she had peeped
into them during her idle moments. Several
were simply journals kept by the lady of the
house, inconsequential and varied, containing
useful recipes for the preserving of game, cheek
by jowl with the news that a neighbour had been
safely delivered of a son; confessing ruefully
that the writer had been sadly dipped at loo the
previous night, or reporting with triumph the
success of a new method of cooking a tough fowl.
Others, kept by the lord of the establishment
or one of his minions, followed a more prosaic
pattern, reporting the success of various crops,
the behaviour of the tenants, and even affairs
of national importance where they affected the
running of the Priory. Alterations and repairs
were carefully recorded, and Katherine had
smiled over a bitter complaint that it was becoming impossible to maintain the south lawn
in its immaculate state, because of a dispute
with regard to a right of way, which the village
folk were defending with vigour and determi-

nation. Perhaps among these uninhibited out-
pourings there might be some reference to the
'Priory' tapestry. One of the journals that had
been kept by a woman, she decided, and there
was one dated about the middle of Queen Eliz-
abeth's reign, or even earlier. The difficulty was
that the journals did not form a complete record.
But she had nearly an hour to spare before the
simple luncheon that Hilda had begged her to
share for the last time. She might as well dip
into one or two of them.

The early volumes were on the very top shelf,
which meant employing the library steps. They
were also thickly coated with dust, since the
shortage of labour made it impossible to keep
the shelves in good order. Katherine picked out
one or two at random, turning the pages briskly,
resisting the temptation to read on and on as
she sought for a reference to the tapestry. There
was nothing. She put back an account of a ban-
quet served to half the countryside in celebra-
tion of the defeat of the Armada, and decided
that there was just time to dip into the next
volume. It followed in chronological order and
was written in the same spidery hand, but although the first few pages turned easily enough,
she had trouble with the middle section. Not to
be defeated she carried it down the steps and
laid it on the table. The pages appeared to be
stuck together. Only the first few and the last
few turned separately. A sudden thought oc-

curred to her. She picked up the volume and shook it. Something within the sealed pages moved. She was sure of it. With infinite care she slid a fingernail under the corner of the first sealed page, thanking Providence that damp had softened the glue, and gently peeled it back. The paper was thick, almost parchment-like which simplified the task, especially as only the edges of the pages had been stuck down. The middle had been cut away to form a cavity some eight inches square. In it lay several small packages wrapped in soft yellowish paper. She did not touch them but went to call Hilda, as certain as a girl could be that she had discovered Mr. Winfield's missing jewels.

FIVE

Jasper was sent home to Hays Park with the
horses and a note for Papa, requesting that the
light chaise should be sent to the Priory to col-
lect his errant daughter. She did not feel that
she could tell Papa the extent of her suspicions
about the mysterious parcels. At present it was
all surmise. She said only that she had made
a discovery that must be communicated to Mr.
Winfield, and that in consequence she might be
a little late in returning home.

She then gave some thought to the problem
of unfolding her story. This was tricky to say

the least of it, since she would have to begin by explaining her presence in the house. Hilda was all for telling the whole story, beginning with the mending of the tapestry and leading up to the discovery of what she, too, was convinced were the missing jewels. Mr. Winfield would be absolutely delighted on all counts, and full of gratitude to his benefactress. Katherine was not so sure. No doubt Mr. Winfield would be very pleased if the parcels did indeed contain the missing jewels. He might be less pleased to discover that he had been entertaining an angel unawares. Seen in retrospect, with the prospect of being obliged to explain her conduct looming ever nearer, she felt that her behaviour had been meddlesome and officious. Mr. Winfield would be well within his rights to resent her interference, however well-intentioned, and to feel that her daily visits had been an unwarrantable intrusion. If that were his reaction, he would find it quite intolerable to be put under a further obligation because she had been instrumental in the recovery of the jewels. She discovered in herself a strong distaste for the whole business, and devoutly wished herself well out of it. A half-hearted suggestion that she should allow Hilda to claim the distinction of making the discovery was indignantly rejected.

"Nobody in his senses would ever believe that I climbed up them steps to look at a lot

of dusty old books," said Hilda practically.
"Besides, credit where credit's due, and it was
you that found them. I daresay you don't want
a grand fuss, but surely you want to see if they
really are the jewels? And it's only decent to
give Mr. Winfield an opportunity of thanking
you."

"Then at least will you help me to conceal my
identity," pleaded Katherine. "Think of the talk
it will make in the neighbourhood if the whole
story comes out. Could you not say that I was
a friend of yours, just visiting you, and that I
mended the tapestry for my pleasure and to pass
the time. It is true enough—and the rest follows
naturally. There is no need to tell him my name,
and I shall be safe away before he thinks to ask.
Then you can tell him that I'm very shy and
don't like to be thanked, and that you promised
faithfully not to tell anyone."

Hilda thought this was a silly idea, and argued that it would be very difficult to refuse
information to her employer, but Katherine
seemed so distressed that she eventually gave
a grudging consent. The interview, which en-
sued when Mr. Winfield came across to the
Priory in response to Hilda's urgent message,
went off much more smoothly than Katherine
had feared. She had taken some pains to ensure
that her own appearance should be as incon-
spicuous as possible. Her gown was the plain
morning one that she kept at the Priory to wear

when she was working, since one could not sit about in riding dress all day; and she took the added precaution of re-dressing her hair in a very severe style that was far from becoming. Her obvious timidity bore out the character that Hilda was to give her, and Hilda herself, garrulous in her excitement, was quite happy to do most of the talking. If Mr. Winfield thought the tale an odd one, he was too kind-hearted to take the nervous little creature to task for her rather encroaching behaviour, and confined himself to hoping that she had not irretrievably damaged the tapestry by her unskilled attentions. He listened patiently to her own rather faltering account of how she had come to examine the old journals, and woke to startled interest when she showed him her discovery.

"So then we thought as how those parcels might have the lost jewels in them, sir," concluded Hilda eagerly. "Won't you please open them and see?"

Mr. Winfield's own heart-beats were not as steady as usual, and he was in no mood to study the reactions of the onlookers. If this odd child really had stumbled across the long lost treasure, then a hundred schemes that had been reluctantly rejected for lack of money to finance them could not be put into operation. From being a continual struggle to make ends meet, life could now offer the fulfilment of his modest dreams. His strong hands shook a little as he picked up the largest parcel and almost fearfully unfolded its dingy wrapping.

There could be no mistaking them. Even in the dimly lit library, the diamonds glowed and sparkled in the candle light. Mr. Winfield held up the necklace, wordlessly, to Hilda's clasped hands and joyous exclamations. Carefully he unwrapped the other parcels. There were more diamonds—a circlet to wear in the hair, two bracelets and several brooches. There was a charming little sapphire pendant, a stone of good colour set in tiny diamonds, and a sapphire and diamond chain. The last two parcels yielded a number of rings and buckles and a gold snuff box.

Mr. Winfield gave a deep sigh of relief from strain, and held out his hand to Katherine. She hesitated briefly before putting her cold little fingers into his clasp, and freed them as soon as she decently could. She was delighted with the outcome of her meddling, but more interested in making her escape. Mr. Winfield—she would not have recognised him, so tall and broad had he grown—picked up the sapphire pendant.

"On your own admission," he said, his voice not quite steady, "it is entirely thanks to you that the jewels have been found. I would like you to accept this as a keepsake, to remind you of a strange adventure, and of the inestimable service that you have rendered me."

Katherine shrank back. "Oh, no sir. No, thank you. I could not. It is reward sufficient to know that I have been of service."

He thought her diffident about accepting a gift of jewellery. "It must be as you wish," he bowed, "but I shall consider this pendant as yours. The other jewels will all be sold. Perhaps you would rather have the price that the pendant will bring."

She did not look the kind of girl who would have much use for a costly jewel, he thought briefly, but if she were in humble circumstances, as her friendship with Hilda would seem to suggest, a respectable sum of money must always be useful.

But the suggestion of financial reward seemed even more distasteful to the girl. She blushed and stammered as she begged him not to think any more about it. She had discovered the jewels by the merest accident, which could have happened to anyone, and could not endure to profit by such a chance circumstance. Mr. Winfield thought her attitude did her credit, and noticed, vaguely, that her speech was quite refined despite her agitation. There was no hurry about the pendant. It could very well wait until they had all had time to recover from so much excitement. No doubt when the girl had had time for sober reflection she would take a more practical attitude. He began to rewrap the jewels, and allowed Hilda and her protegée to withdraw to the housekeeper's quarters. He was not to know that having packed her working equipment in a basket obligingly lent by Hilda, the two of them promptly repaired to the main gateway, where they waited for half an hour in the chilly dusk until the carriage from Hays Park arrived. It had seemed prudent to both that this vehicle should not be permitted to drive up to the house, where it might attract undesirable notice. Their farewell was brief, Hilda anxious to get back to her cosy fireside, Katherine to be on her way. With a promise that once all the fuss and gossip about the recovery of the jewels had died down she would visit Hilda again, she stepped up into the chaise and sank back thankfully against the squabs.

Poor Hilda was obliged to endure a very uncomfortable quarter of an hour with her master on the following morning. That gentleman, in the understandable belief that her young friend was staying in the house, asked when it would be convenient for him to talk with the girl. He not only wanted to discuss the matter of some reward, but also to thank her for the renovation of the Priory tapestry, which he had now had time to inspect. The skill with which the work had been performed came as a surprise, and did more to arouse his curiosity about the needlewoman than had her discovery of his jewels. He also suspected that it had involved weeks of work, and would very much have liked to know how it had been managed without his knowledge.

He came up against a blank wall. Hilda, realising that she could all too easily be trapped into damaging admissions if she volunteered any information whatsoever, stuck firmly to Katherine's own excuse of shyness and a dislike of being thanked.

"And I promised her faithfully, sir, that I wouldn't say who she was or where she came from." And then, suddenly inspired, added, "She said that was the only reward she wanted—no notice taken and no fuss."

In the face of so plain a request, there was nothing that Mr. Winfield could do; but oddly enough the girl's disappearance caused him to think about her a good deal more than her presence had done. Shamefacedly he realised that probably he would not even recognise her if he met her in some place dissociated from the Priory. To be sure, the light had been poor and he had been preoccupied with the jewels, but it was shocking to think that he had paid so little heed to one to whom he was so greatly indebted. He strove to recall her appearance, but the only thing that he could remember clearly was her pleasant speaking voice, which had provided a marked contrast to Hilda's more rustic accents.

He gave up the attempt to summon up a more exact picture of the girl. But when the jewels came to be sold, he kept back the sapphire pendant. He had said he would regard it as hers. Some day, somewhere, he might come across her again. Then they would see.

SIX

After the excitement of her last day at the
Priory, life at Hays Park seemed sheltered but
uneventful. Katherine was thankful enough to
have come off safely from what could have been
an awkward sort of business; but as the days
passed she could not help missing a certain spice
that had put interest into her days at the Priory,
and began to realise how deeply she had been
involved in the life of that ancient establishment. She had only been an onlooker, a listener,
but insensibly she had shared every phase of
the Priory's battle for survival. When crops had
been saved by a lucky spell of fine weather, she
had rejoiced with the workers. When two sturdy

heifer calves had been born on successive days, she had shared the cowman's satisfaction.

At Hays Park, everything was too easy. She tried dutifully to interest herself in the housekeeping and the tenantry. But the housekeeper was no Hilda. She was intimidatingly efficient, and the courteous manner in which she listened to Katherine's occasional suggestions was distinctly chilling. The house ran on oiled wheels. Money, of course, supplied the oil. There were plenty of servants, able-bodied and well-trained. No dust or damp was permitted to encroach here. Naturally Katherine was glad of this, but she missed the stimulus of the alternating victories and disappointments that had coloured life at the Priory. Here, such trivial matters were unimportant.

She also missed, as she confessed to herself with some shame, her own private excitement in doing a good turn by stealth, the fun of staying hidden when the occasional visitor called, and her final satisfaction in concealing her identity and evading the suggestion of reward. This seemed to have been completely successful. It was all the more annoying then that she was left wondering how Mr. Winfield had reacted to her disappearance. Curiosity was a weakness in her, she admitted. She should be satisfied to have made good her escape.

She heard a good deal about present existence at the Priory. The finding of the jewels had been

a nine days' wonder in the neighbourhood, and
speculation as to how the master of the Priory
would make use of his unexpected windfall was
the favourite conversational topic at social
gatherings. It was, perhaps, fortunate that Mr.
Winfield himself, absorbed in disposing of the
jewels to the best advantage, and in setting on
foot certain long-cherished schemes for the future of his estates, was not present at any of
these functions. Tongues were able to wag as
freely as they liked. On the whole they wagged
approvingly. Mr. Winfield was moving slowly,
which appealed to a naturally cautious rustic
community. The only major work on which he
had embarked immediately was the repair of
the Priory roof. He was still living in the bailiff's cottage, though it was understood that he
would move into the big house as soon as repairs
had made it more habitable. A number of new
servants had been engaged, both indoors and
out, and Mr. Winfield had also attended several
cattle sales in the neighbourhood, buying half
a dozen likely looking heifers and a fine young
bull. There was some argument about the wis-
dom of this procedure, one or two of the older
men estimating the cost of a winter's keep for
these animals when feed would be scarce and
expensive, others pointing out that he had
bought them more cheaply because that very
problem had caused other buyers to hang back.
Every one approved the one purchase that

might have been considered extravagant. Mr. Winfield had bought himself a fine upstanding hunter, and it was to be assumed that he would now be seen out occasionally with the local pack.

Since being made privy to his daughter's share in the changing fortunes of the Priory, Mr. Martenhays had taken a keen interest in his young neighbour. He had been told the story under a promise of strict secrecy. He approved her conduct in withdrawing so promptly from the scene of her benevolent activities, and shared her hope that if she should chance to meet Mr. Winfield, he would not recognise her. However, a meeting was not very likely. Katherine had overcome her timidity with horses and rode quite competently, but she still preferred a quiet animal and she did not hunt. Apart from the hunting field or a meeting in going to or from Church, there was little chance of a casual encounter, and Mr. Martenhay's circle of friends was drawn from the older section of the community. Reassured on this head he gave free rein to his interest in Mr. Winfield's doings. He allowed that the hunter was a justifiable extravagance. Though not himself a hunting man, he thought that a young fellow needed some relief from the burden of responsibility imposed by running a large estate. It would do Mr. Winfield good to enjoy a gallop or two, and to get upon friendly terms with his neighbours. But he was much more interested

in his neighbour's schemes for draining a large
area of unproductive wasteland and bringing it
under cultivation. If rumour spoke truth, the
plan was an ambitious one. The drainage would
augment the flow of water in the little river
that ran through the Priory grounds, and Mr.
Winfield was considering the installation of a
water wheel to power a small mill. Generous
marling would improve the quality of the sour
land, and so produce better grazing. This was
the kind of farming practice that Mr. Martenhays understood and approved. To him it rep-
resented a wise investment of capital.

The mill scheme, too, intrigued him. Folk
said that it was to be used for the spinning of
fine woolen yarn, which, in turn, was to be knit-
ted into caps and stockings by workers in the
villages. A trifle quixotic, thought Mr. Martenhays shrewdly, but he could see the boy's idea.
Since so much of the common land had been
enclosed, there had been much hardship among
the labouring classes. There were fewer jobs—
sheep did not need so much tending—and a man
could no longer keep a cow or one or two sheep
of his own to supplement his meagre wage. Such
a mill as Mr. Winfield was proposing might well
fill a useful purpose. It would provide work for
several men, and the knitting would give the
women folk a chance to earn a little money in
their own homes. Whether it would also show

a fair profit on the amount of capital that it
would swallow was a different matter.

Katherine continued to find life a hum-drum
business. It was difficult to win any response
from the labourers and their families. In com-
parison with many of their kind the men were
fairly treated, but they had no real stake in the
land. They were concerned only to do what they
were told and to give satisfaction to the Master.
This attitude they had communicated to their
wives and families. Katherine found them meek
and subservient, agreeing with anything that
she said, humbly grateful for a gift of tea or
soup in case of sickness, but crushed and spir-
itless. The Christmas season with its traditional
celebrations brought a little life to the sedate
cottages, but even then she felt that she knew
their occupants no better. If they were really in
any difficulty they would not dream of bringing
it to the Master's daughter. It might be con-
strued as complaint.

Christmas came and went. January was open
and mild, with a good deal of rain that made
outdoor exercise unpleasant and Katherine
grew more and more restless. Snowdrops came
pricking through the soil, heralding another
spring, but still her life seemed to be drifting
along without purpose. A pale but welcome sun
tempted her out to ride one morning in early
February. She would dearly have loved to visit
Hilda, to hear for herself about the various ac-

tivities at the Priory, but she felt it was too risky. She did not want to chance an encounter with Mr. Winfield just yet. Jasper had told her that there was a meet in the village. She decided to ride that way in the hope of seeing something of the activities, feeling that it would give some purpose to an otherwise aimless ride.

All went well at first. She was riding a new horse, a handsome chestnut gelding named Ajax, a Christmas gift from Papa. Her favourite, Nelly, had an over-reach, but Ajax, though he was bigger and stronger than the mare, had proved himself a very comfortable ride. Unfortunately he also had a will of his own. He had been hunted regularly during the previous season, and had taken to the sport like a duck to water. As the mingled noises of horses, hounds and hunting horn came to his ears, he pricked them forward eagerly. This was something that he knew and understood. He had no notion of being an onlooker. He wanted to be off and away with the leaders, and since his rider seemed to have other ideas, he fought for his head. Jasper came trotting up anxiously to render assistance, but the close approach of another horse seemed to irritate Ajax. He slugged out his head, snatched the bit, and bolted after the vanishing hunt. Katherine could not check his pace. It was all she could do to stay in the saddle, and hope he would tire himself out before she came to grief. A low wall loomed across her path. She

had no chance to steady him and he flew it in
fine style but landed awkwardly, throwing
Katherine clear before galloping off after the
hunt. Jasper and another belated rider jumped
the wall together.

Mr. Winfield, who had promised himself a
day's holiday on this spring-like morning, cursed
heartily. He had already been prevented from
getting to the meet by a minor accident to one
of his men, but had hoped, by taking a short cut
across country, to catch up with the hunt at the
first draw. Chivalry insisted that he should stop
and render what assistance he could. One could
scarcely leave a female lying in a muddy field,
though he did not think that she had come to
much harm. She was already trying to sit up.
Vaguely, he thought that he had seen her somewhere before, though he could not recall her
name. He handed his reins to Jasper and went
to help the lady to her feet. Katherine was
shaken but otherwise unhurt. Her hat had come
off in her fall, and she had a long streak of mud
on one cheek, but apart from that she presented
a charming picture in her beautifully fitting
habit, her hair dressed in the loose ringlets that
were the most comfortable under a hard hat.

Having accepted her assurances that she had
suffered nothing worse than one or two bruises,
and politely restored her hat to her, Mr. Winfield addressed himself to the problem of getting
her home. The simplest way, he suggested, was

for her to ride his horse, which he would lead. It would not be very comfortable, but she could cling to the saddle and he would go very slowly. Her groom could then go off in pursuit of the runaway.

Katherine demurred. "But surely, sir, you came out hunting. I cannot cut up all your plans just because I was so foolish as to permit myself to be thrown. I can easily walk as far as the inn in the village, and there I can hire a conveyance to take me home. Certainly Jasper must go after Ajax, and the sooner the better, but you must not be giving up your day's hunting on my account."

Privately Mr. Winfield endorsed these views, but she seemed a plucky little thing and she had taken the deuce of a tumble. He said politely, "I could not enjoy my sport, ma'am, if I did not first see you safely home. Pray permit me to do so. I think you should be laid upon your bed with some revivifying cordial to calm your nerves, as soon as possible."

He seemed quite determined—and further argument would only waste more time. Katherine capitulated, allowed herself to be lifted on to the back of his tall hunter, and grasped the pommel with one small hand, twisting the other in the animal's mane.

"It's Hays Park, sir. Mr. Martenhay's place," volunteered Jasper. "And I'll be off after Ajax right away, if it please your honour. You can't miss the house. The lodge gates are about half a mile out of the village on the right hand side of the road. But Miss Martenhays will tell you." He touched his hat politely and set spurs to his horse.

Conversation between Mr. Winfield and Miss Martenhays did not flourish. It is an awkward business to lead a horse and talk to its rider, especially when the horse is dancing with impatience for a good gallop, and the rider is none too securely seated. Moreover Katherine was beginning to feel the effects of her fall. Her head ached, and it took all her determination to sit up straight and maintain her precarious balance.

Mr. Winfield was absorbed in his own reflections; Martenhays; he had never met the fellow, though he knew of him as a good employer who treated his workers well. But it was also said of him that he subscribed to a good many modern notions about the ownership of land that went far beyond Dermot's mildly progressive views. Now he supposed that he would be obliged to make his acquaintance. He could scarcely abandon Miss Martenhays on the doorstep.

The meeting did not eventuate. The door was flung open for them by a butler much concerned about his young mistress's unexpected return in such unusual fashion. Dermot, lifting the lady down from her lofty perch, explained the

accident; supported the victim in the view that
it was probably not necessary to send for the
physician, and recommended the healing prop-
erties of a rest and a cup of tea. He then abandoned his charge to the ministrations of the butler, now reinforced by the housekeeper and an
abigail who was presumably the young lady's
maid; said politely that he would do himself the
honour of calling next day to enquire how she
did, and rode down the drive in some relief at
having brushed through a tiresome affair so
easily. It was fortunate that Mr. Martenhays
had not been at home, though they would probably meet on the morrow when he paid his courtesy visit.

Too late to go hunting now, he decided, and
rode home, wondering if he could spare another
day later in the week. Perhaps, if he worked
this afternoon. There was a sheaf of estimates
that he must go through before certain works
could be put in hand. If he made a good start
on those, he might steal a day's hunting on
Thursday.

Once again his intentions were frustrated by
a Martenhays. Katherine's Papa would not permit a day to elapse without expressing his gratitude for Mr. Winfield's services to his daughter.
Upon returning to his home and learning of her
mishap, he did not even stay to take a bite of
luncheon, but had himself driven over to the
Priory immediately.

Despite his annoyance at being interrupted, Dermot liked the warmth and frank manners of his visitor. He shrugged off the gratitude, but kindly, making allowances for the concern of a father, and hoped Miss Martenhays was none the worse for her tumble. Mr. Martenhays reassured him on this head and enquired about his host's schemes for drainage and dam building. The two men were soon happily immersed in the problems that arose over the proper management of a country estate. To a certain extent their views coincided, but Mr. Martenhays shook his head over the number of small farms that made up the Priory estate.

"Too many tenants," he opined. "And half of them, if my own experience is anything to go by, as set in their ways as those old Priory ruins that I passed on my way here. They'll moulder away before they'll change. You'll never make the place pay, farming it in small parcels like that, and neither will your tenants. One large holding is the thing, and plenty of modern implements to do the work."

"And what's to become of my present tenants?" demanded Dermot. "Most of them were born on the place. I've taken two more farms in hand since I took over, and I'll admit that one or two of my tenants are pretty mediaeval in their outlook. But I can't just dispossess them."

"You could employ the willing ones," argued Mr. Martenhays. "They'd be better off with a good master than scratching a poor living as they do now."

"Well there we shall never agree," said Dermot good-humouredly. "However good your employer—and I couldn't afford to be overgenerous—it's not the same thing as being your own master. As the short leases fall in I shall not renew them except in cases of personal hardship, for in theory I agree with your recipe for success. But it will be a long slow business."

Mr. Martenhays grunted. "Too tender-hearted. That's your trouble. It doesn't pay in business. And farming is a business as much as any other."

Dermot's grin was rather rueful. He was very well aware that there was a good deal of sense in his visitor's notions, but he did not see why the fellow should have it all his own way, even though he was an older man and only newly met.

"You bear the reputation, sir, of being a good employer, paying a good wage and caring for your men in time of sickness. Are you asking me to believe that this is just good business practice?" he enquired.

Mr. Martenhays acknowledged the hit. "Perhaps not entirely," he owned with a frosty twinkle. "But I don't carry common decency or Christian charity to the point of endangering my profit. After all—if I go bankrupt, my employees will suffer along with me. It is to their interest that I keep a cool head on my shoulders."

"So much I grant you. But I wonder how you would deal if you found yourself in my situation. I'm no sentimentalist, any more than you are yourself, and I detest idlers and whiners. But when a man and his forefathers have served the land for generations; when tenants are hard workers and honest in all their dealings, would you punish them because their minds are slow moving and do not readily accept new methods?"

Mr. Martenhays scratched his head. "You strike shrewd blows, young man. Though punish is not the word I would use. But this I will say. The new methods must come, however much prejudice there is against them. The population of the country is increasing. With so many more mouths to feed, there's many will starve to death unless we can produce more food. And the old ways cannot do it. You are young. Mark my words, you'll see the changes come quicker and quicker."

Dermot had a pretty shrewd notion that the gentleman was in the right of it, like it or not. In his grandfather's day, the peasants had managed to supply their own needs by working their small holdings, with perhaps a little surplus left in a good season which they would market, to earn the necessary cash to buy such staple commodities as they could not grow for themselves.

Less well informed than Mr. Martenhays, he was still aware that, with the rapid growth of the manufacturing towns and their increasing calls on food supplies, this simple system would no longer meet the nation's needs.

He said quietly, "I have a good deal of sympathy with your views, sir, even if I cannot endorse them wholeheartedly. But so much talk has made me thirsty. Shall we crack a bottle? And then, if you would care for it, I will show you something of the improvements that I am making. I will even promise to listen to your advice, though I do not undertake to accept it as though it were the Gospel."

SEVEN

February gave way to March. One or two early lambs were born, and Dermot moved the lambing flock down to the river pastures where the shepherd could more easily keep an eye on them. Every one grumbled because it rained persistently. The roads and tracks became quagmires, and social life was practically at a standstill.

Sickly weather for the lambing, pronounced the shepherd grumpily. But Dermot had a more pressing anxiety. The progress of his drainage works had already noticeably augmented the volume of the water in the river. Now the heavy rain filled all the little streams to the brim and even caused new springs to break. There was

a threat that the river might burst its banks.
That would put the lambing flock in grave danger, and probably flood several cottages that
stood on the low ground. He arranged for a
watch to be kept on the threatening waters both
day and night, and put extra men to work on
the dam and the mill lade which would eventually divert some of the surplus water but
which, at present, were only half completed.
Those whose houses were threatened were
warned to move their belongings to the upper
floors.

There was a good deal of muttering. The river
had never flooded the houses before. It was all
this drainage business that had turned it into
a menace. One or two wiseacres had known all
along how it would be, and it was no use Sam
Armstrong pointing out that the projected mill
would provide much needed employment. Since
he hoped to be given the job of running it, he
would naturally be in favour, but how would he
like the river coming into his house and spoiling
all his goods? However, having vented their
disapproval, and shown their sour satisfaction
in having been right, they got on with the necessary jobs without further trouble.

Dermot considered his safety measures and
decided that there was no more to be done.
There were two tumble-down shacks on the Island, deserted these many years. The Island was
not really an island. The river looped round it,

almost encircling it, occasionally washing right over it after heavy rain. If, on this occasion, it also washed away the two crumbling buildings, it would be small loss. They were already on Dermot's list for demolition. Travelling tinkers and gypsies had a trick of sheltering there occasionally, with a consequent increase in the petty crime in the district.

On the fourteenth of March, gale force winds brought a lashing rainstorm which precipitated the disaster. For once the wiseacres were wholly justified. Before the drainage scheme it would have taken hours for that volume of water to percolate in the lower levels and bring out the river. Now it flowed rapidly along the carefully dug ditches with nothing to check its onward career. The watchers higher up the valley alerted the Priory workers, while the shepherd and his helpers immediately began to move the flock to higher ground. It was a slow business. The animals could not be hurried for they were heavy in lamb, but they knew their shepherd and made steady progress at their own speed. Dermot went down to the village to see if he could give any help there. Thanks to his precautions there was little more to be done. The water posed no threat to life or limb, and a good neighbourly spirit seemed to have emerged, the old, the sick and the babes having been offered asylum in houses that were not under threat.

Everything was in good hands. He might as well go back and watch developments at the dam.

His foot was actually in the stirrup when one of his tenants called out to him, "Reckon there's some vagrants on the Island, sir. Ben came down that way and said he saw smoke in one of the chimneys this morning."

Dermot put his horse into a gallop. Vagrants were vagrants, and a plaguey nuisance at times, but no one wanted them to run the risk of drowning. Surely men of their experience would have too much sense to camp on the Island when the river was obviously rising.

In this belief he was quite right, but the tinkers, seeing the careful precautions already taken, had counted on being rescued in ample time. That would mean shelter and food for several days, as well as unlimited scope for their pilfering talents. It was worth the risk of a wetting.

So it came about that Katherine, whose Papa had set out a couple of hours earlier with a band of workers to see if he could render any help in village or Priory, came across a band of pitiful refugees, when she rode after him to see how the work was going. The tinkers were hurriedly loading their few oddments into a shabby cart, the women running about distractedly and shouting at the children, most of whom were crying with fright. The piece of land on which the shacks stood was rapidly disappearing be-

neath the encroaching flood waters, and, to
Katherine's tender heart, the group presented
a touching picture of destitution and helplessness.

They were in no actual danger, although the
cart splashed through standing water as it made
for the bank, and the women and children were
ankle deep. There were two or three ponies,
miserable starveling screws to be hauled to
safety. Then the whole band looked expectantly
at Katherine. She did not fail them. Swiftly re-
viewing her resources, she recalled a hay barn,
empty at this season of the year, but sound shelter from wind and rain. To this refuge she directed the sorry crew, promising that hot food
should be provided for them as soon as there
was time for its preparation.

Dermot, arriving in haste at the Island site,
found the place deserted. One of the Hays Park
shepherds who was helping to round up the last
of the sheep, told him what had happened. Annoyance mounted within him. The Island was
a kind of no man's land, neither the Priory nor
Hays Park laying claim to its unprofitable
acres, but since his drainage scheme had been
largely responsible for the flooding, Dermot felt
a certain responsibility for the tinkers. His reaction would have been to give them a good
meal and a small sum of money and to send
them on their way. If Miss Martenhays had offered them shelter they would undoubtedly bat-

ten on her hospitality until even her patience was exhausted. He would be obliged to ride over and discover if he could render her any assistance; probably in ridding her of a bunch of arrant knaves, he thought savagely. But the matter would have to wait. There were more urgent tasks awaiting his supervision.

Thanks to sensible precautions, and the help of willing hands, they survived the flood without loss of stock or injury to the workers. There was a good deal of mess to be tidied up in the cottages that had been invaded by the muddy water, and one or two items of household goods had been overlooked and so spoiled or washed away, but on the whole there was singularly little damage. Mr. Winfield, having inspected the work that was in progress, and tactfully disbursed small sums of money for the replacement of essential items, decided next day that he could be spared to ride over to Hays Park to thank Mr. Martenhays for the speed and efficiency with which he had rendered assistance, and to enquire into the position with regard to the tinkers. He found Mr. Martenhays from home, he having been called unexpectedly to London for an important conference. Though nominally retired, his associates still relied upon his experience and judgement in matters of great moment. Miss Martenhays, said the butler, with that air of complete impersonality that indicates deep disapproval, was gone across to the barn where the tinkers were lodged. One of the children was sickly, it appeared; and she had ignored all the representations of himself and the housekeeper, to the effect that she was like to catch a pestilent fever by meddling with such low trash, and had gone to see if she could be of help. In the absence of her father there was no one to gainsay her, he added, and looked hopefully at Mr. Winfield as though he might be just the man to do it.

The scene that met Mr. Winfield's eye when he went into the barn was much what he had expected. Naturally there was no fireplace, but two braziers had been lit, and lent something of an air of comfort to the big bare place. The tinkers had added their own note of disorder. A cord had been stretched from wall to wall, and an array of tattered garments had been spread out to dry. The men of the party were missing—it might be better not to enquire what they were about—save for one middle-aged fellow who, in a rather desultory fashion, was effecting rough and ready repairs to some harness. One woman was tending something in a pot slung over one of the braziers; two more were engaged in acrimonious dispute over the possession of a red shawl, each declaring that it was her shawl that had survived the hurried evacuation of the Island; while a fourth was crouching over a makeshift crib in which lay the object of Katherine's concern.

To visit her unsavoury protegées, Katherine had donned that plain morning gown that had been her working dress at the Priory, and had dressed her hair close to her head. As she glanced up from the baby, at the opening of the door, Dermot recognised her at once. It was the girl of the jewels and the tapestry. With that serious, concerned expression on her face there was no mistaking her. She was also, undoubtedly, Miss Martenhays.

For a moment Mr. Winfield forgot all about the debt of gratitude that he owed her. He was swept by a wave of primitive fury at the thought that this child of wealth and privilege should have run tame at the Priory for weeks, privy to all the shifts and subterfuges that poverty had forced upon him. Mrs. Armstrong's 'friend' indeed! 'Gifted with her needle and thankful to earn her board by plying it.' For that one furious moment he could cheerfully have wrung the girl's neck.

His rage was swiftly brought under control, but his greeting was distinctly stiff. Katherine, unaware of his recognition, and remembering his kindness after her fall from Ajax, welcomed him with unaffected cordiality. To speak the truth she was very glad to see him. The tinkers made her feel uneasy. They were shameless beggars, claiming to have lost food supplies, clothing and household goods in the flooded river, in such quantities as would have furnished a substantial house. Having been on the scene herself, and watched their belongings being loaded into the cart, she knew that the claims were quite without foundation; but a generous heart found excuse for some degree of imposition from people so abjectly poor. It was not this, so much as their manner of approach, that distressed her. This varied from sycophantic gratitude, expressed in such flowery terms as to be totally unconvincing, to a kind of veiled insolence that would have been alarming if she had not been on her own ground with servants within call. Even as matters stood she was aware of the comfort of masculine support.

"I will walk back to the house with you," she said hospitably. "Papa has been called away, but you must take some refreshment before you go." She turned back for a moment to the tinker woman. "I will send some milk for the little boy," she promised, as the big barn door was flung open and an irate Jasper appeared on the threshold, followed by one of the stable boys.

"By your leave, Miss Katherine," he jerked out. "There's a whole heap of tackle gone missing. I had it spread out on the bench in the harness room, all ready for cleaning, when I was called away to help fig out the master's carriage. When I went back, there was a headpiece missing and some girths and traces. I'm just wondering if any of them's found their way down here."

The tinker looked up from his task with all the resignation of one who is accustomed to being falsely accused. "Search if you please," he said indifferently. "You'll find no harness here, save our own bits and pieces."

Dermot thought that was probably true. It was pretty certain that the tinkers knew all about the missing tackle, but they were too wily to have hidden it where the most superficial search must discover it at once. It was probably already tucked away under some hedge, where they could pick it up at their leisure after leaving the precincts of Hays Park. No wonder that the tinker appeared quite unperturbed by Jasper's methodical search. The only suspicious article that was found in the cart was a bucket— which Jasper had not even missed—half full of corn. But the man said it was to feed the horses, and that he had put it in the cart to prevent them from getting at it unbeknownst. It might have been true, though Dermot wondered cynically when those miserable broken down animals had last tasted corn. Certainly no one could disprove it.

The tinker, however, had reckoned without his female colleagues. Jasper, flushed and annoyed at having failed to make good his case in front of his young mistress and Mr. Winfield, made a last desperate cast. He bent over the basket which was serving as a crib for the tinker baby, handed the child to its mother and lifted out the bedding. Underneath lay a bundle wrapped in a towel, which, upon being unrolled revealed not, indeed, the missing harness, but a collection of spoons and knives, a small silver mug that Katherine had used as a child, and a scarf that she did not even know she had lost.

The tinker mother burst into voluble explanation, but Dermot cut her short. "Best leave me to deal with this," he told Katherine. "And you—Jasper, is it? Take these things up to the house. Do you want to bring the law into the business?" he went on, turning back to Katherine.

She shook her head, unable to trust her voice in her distress at having been made to look so foolish.

"Very well. Then if you, too, will go back to the house, I'll get rid of these rogues for you."

Katherine went meekly enough, though she felt some resentment at this high-handed dealing. One of the older women began to whine about having nowhere to go. "There's cruel you are," she told Dermot reproachfully, "turning women and children out into the storm, and Eily there with a sick wean."

Dermot hid a grin for her impudence. "It seems to have escaped your attention, granny, but the sun is shining. However, if you insist on shelter you may lie snug enough at the nearest round house. I'll get Miss Martenhays to lay an information against you."

The old dame swore at him with vigour and freedom, but he said only that they might think themselves fortunate that the lady they had imposed upon was of so kindly a disposition; and she began reluctantly to gather clothing together and bundle it into the cart, not forgetting to curse the woman called Eily for being unable to keep her fingers from picking and stealing for a few days longer. "T'wouldn't have hurt you to wait," she grumbled. "We could have lain here snug for a week with all our food given us, and plenty of gleanings from the fat farm lands."

Strolling up to the house, with a final injunction to the stable boy to oversee the rest of the packing and escort the party off the premises, Dermot felt himself slightly more in charity with Miss Martenhays. He had not done very much, but he had lent her his support in an uncomfortable situation. His debt to her did not seem quite so burdensome, and although he could not entirely bring himself to forget the way in which she had insinuated herself into the Priory, it seemed to make matters better that he had seen her taken completely at fault. Women, he thought. Sweet and soft and gullible; but he thought it kindly, for little Miss Martenhays had looked rather charming in her embarrassment.

Katherine's own feelings were divided. On the one hand she was grateful to the gentleman

for the masterful way in which he had dealt
with the tinkers, yet at the same time, she had
not liked feeling small and foolish in his eyes.
Papa had already taken her to task for her impulsive folly in offering to shelter the tinker
clan, and had warned her of its probable outcome; so she was sensitive to further criticism.
Not that it was Mr. Winfield's place to criticise
any of her actions, she decided, putting up her
chin. She found it soothing to her sore pride that
he did not even refer to the tinker incident, but
spoke instead of the prompt help that her father
had furnished during the flooding; passing naturally enough to the present state of affairs in
the village, the tale enlivened by one or two
small comical incidents that had occurred during the hurried selection and packing of household treasures before they were swept away.

By the time that he referred to their meeting
on the morning that Ajax had thrown her, they
were getting on quite comfortably together, and
she answered his interested enquiries about
Ajax readily enough, explaining about Nelly's
lameness on that particular day. In fact, she felt
herself so much in charity with him for not teasing her over her misguided benevolence, that
she actually reminded him of that long ago incident of their first meeting; explaining how she
had named Nelly for "The first horse that did
not terrify me," his own much loved mare. For-
tunately Dermot remembered it too, and they

spent some time in discussing the recent history of the Dorsey family. Dermot was no hypocrite to dress up unpalatable facts prettily because convention demanded that he speak well of the dead. He said, frankly, that young Thomas had only come by his just deserts. "A sad waste of a life," he said curtly. "Spoiled from babyhood because he was the heir. Heir to debts and mortgaged estates, decayed farms and tumbledown buildings," he put in bitterly. "And encouraged to think that his overbearing ways were manly."

He realised that youthful memories of those overbearing ways had caused him to speak more harshly than was perhaps just, so he added apologetically, "I need not stand upon points with you. Perhaps I exaggerate, but you yourself suffered at the hands of that pretty pair, so you will understand what I mean."

"I certainly suffered at Emma's," smiled Katherine, now feeling quite at ease. "She always blamed me for the fact that they were found out that day, though actually it was none of my doing. Someone had seen them in the village, and had told the Countess. I don't suppose she minded about my being neglected," she elaborated, "but she was furious that her orders had been disobeyed. I was truly thankful when Emma left school."

"She seems to be pretty comfortably established now," said Dermot thoughtfully. "At least I suppose it suits her. Heaven knows she had plenty of offers. But old Perceval is as rich as Midas and dotes on her, so I presume she is satisfied with her bargain."

Under this easy exchange of views Katherine had grown so relaxed that she did not stop to think. "It would not do for me," she said slowly. "To be married for one's money is quite bad enough. When there is such disparity of age as well, it must disgust any one of principle."

The words were scarcely uttered before she realised what she had said and flushed scarlet, her fingers flying to her lips. To utter such scathing condemnation of one who was related to her listener was scarcely the behaviour of a well-bred hostess. For a moment she was irrationally angry with Dermot because his easy manners had led her to speak her mind without thought. But he was swift to recognise her embarrassment, and to soothe it.

"Well you must agree that it is impossible to imagine Emma married to a poor man," he pointed out, reasonably enough. "I should be very sorry for the gentleman concerned if that were the case. But enough of the Dorseys. When are you going to persuade your Papa to bring you over to see the alterations that I am putting in hand at the Priory? I would be glad of your advice as to which of the hangings and tapestries are worth repairing, and which are damaged beyond recovery. Which reminds me, Miss Martenhays, that I have a crow to pluck with you. You vanished so promptly and so completely after your discovery of the jewels that almost I began to wonder if you were the good fairy who figures so prominently in nursery tales. Luckily, Hilda was able to reassure me as to your existence, though she would tell me nothing else. And somehow, somewhere I felt that we would meet again. You could not have been permitted to bestow such benefits upon me and then go out of my life completely. I confess, however, that I did not recognise you at first. It was only when I saw you in the barn this morning that I realised you were my shy benefactress. You may like to know, however, that you were not forgotten. I kept the sapphire pendant when I disposed of the other jewels. As I told you, I counted it yours. For the second time I humbly beg you to accept a simple keepsake of the whole bizarre incident."

Katherine lost herself in a tangle of half sentences. She did not wish for reward. Every feeling must rebel. It would be quite improper to accept a gift of valuable jewellery from one who was not a relation. She had taken great delight in her work on the tapestry, and the discovery of the jewels was purely fortuitous.

Dermot listened gravely until she ran out of breath. Then he said pleasantly, "As for the impropriety of accepting a gift of jewellery from a gentleman, I think that your Papa must be the judge of that. Does he know the circumstances?"

Katherine nodded dumbly.

"Then we shall ask his permission. I do not think that he will refuse it. I am happy to hear that you enjoyed your work on the tapestry, since it encourages me to hope for your advice in the future. Your other arguments are absurd, and you know it. If your Papa agrees to it, will you accept my pendant?"

She made one last attempt. "But do you not see, I could not possibly wear it? How if I were to meet the Countess or Emma, and they were to recognise it as family jewellery?"

He gave her the kind of tolerant smile that a benevolent uncle might have bestowed upon a rather dim niece. "My dear girl!" He, too, had forgotten to mind his tongue. "The jewels have been missing for some fifty years. Emma, certainly, could never have seen them. The Dowager"—his mouth curved in amusement— "will certainly never admit to having done so, unless it was in her cradle. There can be no one alive today who could actually identify one insignificant pendant."

Driven against the wall, she said stubbornly, "Is it not enough that I do not wish to accept it?"

He looked at her steadily for a long moment. Her head was well up and she returned his gaze without flinching.

"No," he said deliberately. "It is not. I did not wish to have an unknown female insinuating herself into my house. Spying out the poverty of the land, for all I know; mending my cherished tapestry—beautifully, I admit, but without my knowledge or consent. The discovery of the jewels I cannot resent, since it has enabled me to do so much for the estate and all who are bound up in it. But that, by your own admission, was purely accidental. Since I was obliged to accept your intrusion into my affairs, I think that you should pay forfeit by accepting the pendant."

He saw the irresolution in her face and hastened to throw in a clincher. "I daresay your jewel case is amply stocked, Miss Martenhays, but surely you could find room in it for one more small trifle."

It was enough. The suggestion that she was so high-nosed as to despise his jewel brought her to submission. If she were honest she could have told him that the sapphire pendant would remind her of pleasant useful days which held a faint spice of excitement. She would like nothing better than to accept it if she might properly do so.

"Very well, sir," she said, stiffly formal. "I will agree to abide by Papa's decision." And bade him a cool good morning.

EIGHT

Mr. Martenhays roundly informed his daughter that she was being foolish beyond permission. There was no reason why she should not yield to Mr. Winfield's wishes, since he felt so strongly on the matter. It was only natural that he should wish to make some gesture of appreciation, and surely the gift of one of the romantically discovered jewels was just the thing to appeal to a sentimental female heart. Its value was of no particular consequence—when one was as wealthy as Mr. Martenhays it was easy to take a large-minded view of such matters—and as for propriety, only the three of them would know of the gift, and Winfield was certainly not the type of fellow to brag about it.

Katherine yielded to the view of the majority and accepted the pendant with an outward show of decorous but restrained appreciation. Secretly, it delighted her. She loved everything about it, from its faded velvet case and antique setting to the deep blue fire of the central stone. She wondered why she had never thought to choose sapphires among the many trinkets that her father had bestowed upon her. To be sure, she did not often wear blue, Aunt Julia having declared that it was a colour more suited to a blonde, while she was beech-nut brown. Her eyes were blue, though. Or it might be more truthful to admit that they were of that indeterminate shade of blue-grey that could look blue in certain lights and certain moods. They looked blue when she wore the pendent; and wear it she did, though never in public. Often at night, her maid dismissed, she would take it out of her jewel box and clasp it about her throat. But despite these private sessions of gloating, despite the pendant's manifest suitability for modest functions, such as the informal evening gatherings with which the country gentry beguiled the time now that the roads were passable once more, she could not bring herself to wear it when she was likely to meet Mr. Winfield. And she met him more and more frequently as the weeks passed. There might be a whist party, for the devotees, with some hilarious round game for the younger guests. Sometimes they would dance—eight or nine couples performing country dances and the occasional quadrille with more enjoyment than artistry; or there would be music and charades. Katherine found herself enjoying these simple rustic festivities with considerably more enthusiasm than she had recently brought to the far more polished entertainment offered to her in Town. She even acknowledged—to herself—that the presence of Mr. Winfield at a good many of them added just that degree of piquancy that lifted them above the commonplace. She danced with him; played loo and charades with him; permitted him to turn over her music when she found herself unable to escape the obligation of playing for the company; but she would not wear his pendant. To do so, would be to give him best in the silent duel of wills that was still being fought between them behind the polite social façade.

Even apart from social encounters she saw a good deal of Mr. Winfield. Her father regarded him as a promising convert to his own notions of modern farming, and was forever inviting him to Hays Park to see some new machine in action, or to seek his advice on the selection of stock, where, he frankly admitted, the younger man was his master.

"We ought to work in partnership," he announced one day. "Between us we'd clean up a handsome fortune."

These sessions with the agricultural mysteries usually ended with the pair of them coming back to Hays Park, muddy and contented, despite their fierce arguments; extremely thirsty and often hungry, too. Katherine grew accustomed to her father's demands for tankards of ale at unseasonable hours, and his requests that another cover should be set at their dinner table. She told herself that she was glad that he found so congenial a friend with whom to share his interests. More and more often she rode with him when he went over to the Priory, giving her views on the restoration work that was in progress when they were requested, spending a comfortable hour cosing with Hilda when the men were engrossed with farming matters.

If Hilda was busy, she would amuse herself by strolling through the big bare rooms, planning how she would furnish and decorate them if they were hers. As an invited guest she was free of the whole house, and she explored it thoroughly. That was delightful, but it was frustrating to have to keep her eager fingers from attempting the dozens of tasks that challenged the skilled needlewoman. It was abundantly plain that for years there had been a sad lack of household management at the Priory. In the days of its affluence, anything that was a little worn or damaged had been relegated to the lumber room in the attics. In the lean years, when expensive replacements became impossible, there had still been no attempt at the repairs that could have prolonged the life of curtains and hangings. Matters were a little better under the present regime, but most of Mr. Winfield's time and care were still devoted to his outdoor pursuits. Mr. Martenhays approved such conduct— long-headed, he pronounced. Naturally the land must come first. Katherine, however, held that the house merited a larger share of its owner's attention. Indoors there was no one to see what needed to be done and arrange for the necessary attention. From this, it was but a short step to the discovery that what Mr. Winfield required was a wife. She left off furnishing his rooms and set herself to list the salient features of a suitable helpmeet for him.

She would have to be a woman of character— in fact distinctly strong-minded. Otherwise she would never be able to hold her own against the determined Mr. Winfield, decided Katherine, still smarting from her defeat in the matter of the pendant. On the same grounds, it would probably be better if she were not in her first youth. Yes, certainly better. A young girl would expect him to be dancing attendance on her, when any one could see that he was much too busy. She must be a capable housekeeper, too, accustomed to the management of a large household, with a due eye to economy. And speaking of economy, it would be a good thing if she was possessed of a handsome portion. The

Priory could use all the money it could lay its hands on.

At which point in her musings she pulled herself up short, a little aghast to realise that she was actually suggesting that Mr. Winfield should find himself an heiress. She—with her views on marrying for money! She made her way back to the housekeeper's room in a rather subdued frame of mind, though she could not forbear a chuckle at the thought of the intimidating creature whom she had conjured up to be Mr. Winfield's bride.

Oddly enough, Mr. Winfield himself had been giving some thought to the subject of marriage. His views were a good deal less prosaic than Katherine's. In fact, in only one respect did his ideas of a suitable bride agree with hers. He wanted a woman of character. The woman he would choose was a gentle creature, diffident and retiring, who reminded him a little of his mother; but for all her shyness she had a will of her own and a delicacy of principle that he respected, even when it caused her to cross his will. Well—he had overborne her on that one occasion, even if he had been obliged to enlist her father's support to help him to do it. The encounter had left him with a strong desire to establish his mastery over her once and for all. Not that he would dream of bullying or coercing her, except perhaps for a little coercion by way of love play. Once or twice, when they had danced together and she had moved in docile fashion at his bidding, he had wondered how she would react if one day he ventured to steal a kiss. It would be easy to prison the slender wrists in one hand, and to tilt her face to his with the other. She was so small and slight that physically she would be helpless against him. Would those great luminous eyes scorch him with their angry scorn, or would she yield to his embrace and return his kiss?

He would never know, because it was only an idle dream. The devil of it was that after going heart-whole all these years he must needs fall in love with an heiress; one, moreover, who had the lowest opinion of fortune hunters, as he had heard from her own lips. He supposed he might describe himself as a man of modest means—and even that degree of comfort he owed largely to his little love. If she had not chanced upon those jewels it would still be make-and-scrape with him. Even as matters stood, it must be several years—and years of good fortune at that—before he could consider himself safely established. The Priory must be a drag on him for some time to come, since he could not bring himself to initiate the sweeping reforms that Mr. Martenhays recommended at the expense of his poorer tenants. He would introduce them gradually, as opportunity offered, but it might take years, and one could not expect a girl to wait indefinitely to settle her affairs, especially a girl who had been one of the ornaments of London society since her come-out, and who must have recieved any number of more brilliant offers. Meanwhile, he must endure the growing intimacy that his friendship with her father engendered. It was a bitter-sweet business, having the girl you loved strolling about the house and grounds that you also loved, and telling you just how to set it off to its best advantage if only you had the money to pay for such nonsense. Not that it was nonsense, of course. He would dearly have loved to furbish up the old place just as she suggested, for her tastes marched with his. Then he would have offered it—and himself—for her acceptance.

Well—that was not possible. He had been perfectly frank in his talk, both with the girl and her father. They knew his financial circumstances almost as well as he knew them himself. If he were to offer for her now, who could believe him to be disinterested?

It was not too difficult to see the thing sensibly in the privacy of his library. He must put the thought of Katherine Martenhays from him, for she was above his touch. It was less easy when they were thrown together half a dozen times a week. Katherine had always been one to rate her own attractions very modestly. She knew that in point of looks she was no more than well to pass, well to her only striking feature being those magnificent eyes. For the rest her charm was the timid appeal of some shy woodland plant, shrinking into insignificance in competition with more flamboyant flowers. The difference now lay in her closer acquaintance with Mr. Winfield. They had come to know each other so easily, so naturally, and they had so many common interests, that she was no longer shy and stiff with him. She had no idea how her innocent confidence in his pleasure at each new meeting, her smile of welcome or the tiny gesture of a slim hand across a crowded room, transformed her normal rather sober bearing to warm young gaiety. No idea, either, how it bewitched the earnest agriculturist who stood so high in Papa's esteem. Mr. Winfield, whose quiet, stay-at-home ways had made him the despair of all the marriageable maidens in the neighbourhood, fell into the habit of accepting every invitation which gave him the chance of meeting Miss Martenhays, and became adept in calculating which these were. It was not sensible behaviour for a man already deeply in love. Every meeting served to strengthen the attachment, showing him some new aspect of his lady love that enmeshed him more securely. Best of all was the day when she rode up to the Priory with only Jasper in attendance, bringing a message from Papa excusing himself from an engagement that they had made. Mr. Martenhays had taken a slight chill, and since he had a bronchial tendency, it

seemed wiser for him to stay indoors. Dermot
chanced to be conferring with Hilda in the hall,
and persuaded the unexpected visitor to take a
glass of sherry wine before she rode back to
Hays Park; and the two of them strolled together through rooms that already showed the
improvement wrought by assiduous polishing,
discussing the sort of furniture that would best
replace the pieces removed by the Countess. It
was just such a conversation as might have been
shared by a betrothed pair planning their new
home, and they enjoyed it very much.

But it gave Katherine seriously to think.
Dressing for an evening party, happily planning
what she would say to Mr. Winfield about the
planting of the herb garden, it was suddenly
borne in upon her that more and more of her
time was becoming involved with that gentleman and his affairs. The more she thought
about it the more alarmed she became, for she
realised that she had been more absorbed and
happy during the past weeks than at any time
since she had made her come out. And all that
contentment stemmed from one source. Surely
she could not be developing a tendre for a
gentleman whose behaviour towards her varied
from the fraternal to the avuncular? She was
not without experience. She knew very well how
gentlemen behaved when they wanted to fix
their interest with a lady, or even to indulge in
less serious gallantries. Mr. Winfield's behav-

iour was not in the least like that. Sometimes
they discussed things amicably enough, at others they argued or joked each other. But there
had never been any hint that he admired her,
still less that she stirred his pulses. She was
sorely perplexed, not wishing to forfeit her pleasure in his society, but fearful of becoming too
deeply involved.

So it was that, when a letter arrived from
Aunt Julia begging her to spend a few weeks
in Town, she decided to accept. She did not
really want to go, but the effort required to tear
herself away frightened her even more. At least
the visit would give her a short breathing space
away from Mr. Winfield's beguiling influence.

Aunt Julia's welcome was warm and heartening, and since she had already spread the
word of Katherine's impending visit, there were
several invitations awaiting the girl's attention.
There was also a charming posy from Lord Sandiford who had called that very morning to enquire the precise date of her return to civilisa-
tion.

"His words, not mine," added Aunt Julia. "So
I daresay we shall have him running in and out
of the house at all hours. But it won't do, my
love. I have it on good authority that he is all
to pieces. A pity, for he is a most likeable creature and extremely well-connected besides; but
there it is. Your Papa would never give his consent."

Katherine said that while she had always found his Lordship an entertaining companion she had never for a moment taken him seriously, a fact of which he was perfectly well aware, and went on to discuss plans for the month ahead.

It proved to be a busy one. Although it was still early in the Season there was no lack of variety in Katherine's programme, and whether or no Lord Sandiford stood in imminent danger of arrest for debt, as Lady Julia warned, he was still her most assiduous escort. He could still provide a very dashing curricle and pair to take her driving in the Park. She rode or walked with him at other times, danced with him at the Assemblies and accepted his invitation to make one of a theatre party. Aunt Julia protested that she was encouraging his attentions beyond what was seemly, but Katherine retorted that Julian was very well aware that she had nothing for him beyond friendship.

"Then to be calling him by his given name shows a degree of intimacy that I cannot approve," said Lady Julia crossly, and went off to write to 'Cousin John', and to pour out her concern over his daughter's uncharacteristic behaviour.

Her letter annoyed its recipient considerably and produced an unexpected result. Behind the genial frankness of his manners, Mr. Martenhays had a very acute mind. He would have been the first to acknowledge that without it he could never have attained the heights of success that he had achieved in his profession, far less accumulated his immense fortune. And he would have added that there was no need to go about looking gimlet-eyed and tight-lipped in order to convince people of one's shrewdness. One could be perfectly pleasant and affable, and business dealings went all the better for that, too. Much of his success was founded on a good understanding of his fellow men, and his one weakness, if he had one, was his inability to restrain his impatience when they were slow to accept ideas that he was convinced would benefit them in the long run.

Recently he had begun to fancy himself in the rôle of Eros. Quite early in their acquaintance the idea had occurred to him that young Winfield might be just the man for Katherine. He had been at some pains to pursue the connection—all in the most open and natural way—and his first impressions were confirmed. The lad had a few sentimental notions that prevented him from yielding wholeheartedly to the modern methods of farming that the older man advised, but Mr. Martenhays, himself a kindhearted man, could understand and sympathise with his reluctance to uproot the frail and elderly. Time would eventually attend to that, and Mr. Martenhays respected his young friend's decision to leave it so. In every other way he

showed promise of being an ideal son-in-law. He
was intelligent and hard-working, and did not
squander his blunt on gaming or racing. He enjoyed a mug of ale but he was temperate in both
eating and drinking. And he was well-born,
coming from the same class as Katherine's long-
dead Mama. Mr. Martenhays admitted that,
providing everything else was in tune, he would
like to see his girl marry into the landed gentry.
He did not know how Winfield appeared to feminine eyes, but he was a well set up sort of man,
good looking enough in a high-nosed sort of way,
and pleasant-mannered with it. Apart from that
one tiff over the pendant, he and Katherine had
appeared to get along pretty comfortably together. He himself, he felt, had indicated his
approval when he had said that he and Winfield
ought to go into partnership. If the young man
could not accept so broad a hint, he was more
of a slowtop than Mr. Martenhays had reckoned
for. His daughter he had assessed rather better.
He believed that she had gone off to London to
make up her mind. After all, even though Winfield and the Priory seemed to her father to offer
her precisely the kind of life that would suit
her, it was a big decision to make. Marriage
lasted a long time. She was wise to draw off for
a while to think it over.

But this letter of Julia's was another pair of
shoes. No young rakeshame, however charming, was going to marry his daughter. Had the

girl run mad? Or had she and Winfield quarrelled so disastrously that she was seeking any kind of balm for her hurts? It might be sensible to ride over to the Priory and see if he could pick up a hint as to how matters stood.

But although he was Dermot's master in business affairs, and even in some matters concerning the wise management of land, in matters of the heart he was the merest amateur. Dermot betrayed nothing, save a natural and friendly interest in Miss Martenhays's sojourn in the Metropolis, expressing the hope that she was enjoying all the amenities that were so sadly lacking in rustic circles. The exchange ended with an exasperated Mr. Martenhays revealing a good deal more than he had intended. The very fact that Mr. Winfield did not press him for his confidence made him more expansive.

"There's one amenity that I for one could well dispense with," he grunted savagely. "She seems to be encouraging the attentions of a handsome, useless fribble. According to her aunt's account, he haunts the place. Young Sandiford. You'll have heard of him, maybe, though I reckon he's an older man than you. Been on the Town ever since he was sent down from Oxford, and if there's any foolish, mischievous prank that he hasn't tried, it's because he's never heard of it. Gaming, racing, boxing the watch, squandering his blunt on any reckless wager that took his fancy, though, to give him his due, he did steer clear of the Hellfire Club. Up to his ears in debt, of course. That goes without saying. And to be making up to my girl! It's her money he's after. You can lay your life on that."

He paused for breath, mopped a heated brow, and realised that he had been more than a little indiscreet.

"Shouldn't have told you any of this," he muttered apologetically. "Other people's troubles a dead bore. 'Specially when there's nothing you can do to help. But it has helped, just spilling it all out to you, if that's any excuse. The thing that puts me all on end is the fellow's uselessness. I wouldn't mind that he owed money for the shirt on his back if the back had ever been bent in honest toil. I've nothing against a poor man. Often thank God that I was never poor myself, for I was born into the world hosed and shod, as they say, though I make no pretentions to gentle blood. Merchant stock, and comfortable with it. My wife was gently born. Pluck to the backbone, too, or she'd never have stuck to her promise and married me in the face of her parents' opposition. Katherine is like her in looks. Fragile and gentle. But until now I've always thought she resembled me in mind and character. She's a worker, my Katherine, and shrewd, for a female. Wants to be of some use in the world. What would she do with a smart husband who has no higher ambition than to set a fashion in waistcoats, or the proper tying of a neckcloth, or to kick up foolish larks to vent his superabundant energies? If she imagines that such a one would suit her, she must be all about in her head."

Dermot suppressed his own deep dismay at this report, and returned a soothing answer. It was years since he had spent a Season in Town, but he well remembered the place as a hotbed of gossip. Small incidents were exaggerated out of all proportion.

"One cannot blame this gentlemen for paying his addresses to Miss Martenhays," he pointed out. "She is a most attractive young lady, with none of the ridiculous affectations that spoil so many of our fashionable beauties. Small wonder that she is a social success. It is perfectly possible that this Viscount Sandiford is genuinely attached to her, in which case he may be eager and willing to change his way of life."

"Eager and willing's one thing. Determined and persevering's another," growled Mr. Martenhays. "No doubt he'd be full of fair promises. Probably he'd mean 'em at the time. But once the knot was tied and he could hang up his debts to my account, how long d'you think his good resolutions would last? He's not a half broke youngster. He's a man of the world; set in his ways."

Dermot was silenced. Presently Mr. Martenhays went on more quietly, "It's not as though I couldn't stand the nonsense. I'd spend every penny I have to see my girl happy. But she wouldn't be. She's a careful, thoughtful girl. Silly at times, of course, as females are. Look at that business with those damned tinkers! But down at heart she's sensible enough. She'd not like to see my hard-earned money frittered away on the kind of excesses to which young Sandiford is given."

There was a brief silence. He stood up, finished his wine, and said, with a half reluctant laugh, "I have surely betrayed my merchant blood. Not that I care about it, with you. You work as hard for your incomings as ever I did, so you understand. It's not the money itself, but the greed for it; in those who do not know what work means. That is what frightens me. That is what I resent."

Mr. Winfield persuaded him to stay to supper, but none of his comforting remarks about the good sense to be expected of Miss Martenhays, or the character of Lord Sandiford, were successful in cheering his guest. He waved him away as dusk was falling, genuinely sorry for as likeable a man as he had ever met.

NINE

Once the distraction of Mr. Martenhays's presence was removed, it did not take Dermot long to come to a decision. Never mind the work that he had planned for the next week or two. He would go up to Town and see for himself the style of this Viscount Sandiford who aspired to marry the girl that he loved. He might turn out to be a decent sort of fellow; in which case he, Dermot, would be obliged to resign himself to acceptance of Katherine's choice. But if he turned out to be the fortune-hunting loose-screw of Mr. Martenhays's gloomy prognostications, then the girl would have to be protected against herself. He was not quite sure how he would set about it, but somehow he would put a spoke in the fellow's wheel.

He would have to put up at an hotel, not being possessed of that expensive luxury, a house of his own in Town. Fenton's would serve. He remembered it as comfortable enough, and in any case, if he meant to follow the social round he would see very little of it! Which reminded him that he must look up one or two old friends and enlist their good offices to get himself invited to some of the *ton* parties, where he might expect to see Katherine and her beau. He did not anticipate any difficulty there. Though it was some years since he had graced the social scene, there were friends of his mother's who would give him a kindly welcome for her sake.

Matters fell out much as he had expected. The arrival of a new and reasonably eligible bachelor in polite circles was greeted with acclaim. Old friends remembered him, and put the word about. By the end of the week he had a list of engagements that would have done credit to an habitué, and he had made the acquaintance of Viscount Sandiford.

If Katherine had not been involved in the matter, Dermot would have dismissed the Viscount as quite a pleasant sort of fellow, perfectly at home on any sporting suit, if a bit of a lightweight when it came to serious affairs. Speculation was rife as to his chances of success with "the heiress". The majority held that these were good. This was Katherine's fourth Season. She must surely be concerned to find a husband soon, unless she wanted to end up an ape leader. Apart from his debts and his expensive habits Lord Sandiford was quite a creditable *parti*. There were some, however, who stood to it that the girl would never have him, pointing out that he had made all the running during the previous summer but the affair had fizzled out with the ending of the Season. Dermot took what comfort he could from these few. It was true that Katherine was seen a good deal in Sandiford's company, but Dermot did not think that her manner showed anything more than liking for a pleasant escort. In fact, the greeting that she extended to himself showed an equal warmth.

She teased him a little, declaring that he was quite the last person that she had expected to see in Town, and wondering how the heifers and the hay crop were getting on in the absence of the master; but she was perfectly happy to dance with him, to drive out with him, and to accept his escort to various entertainments including a masquerade at Covent Garden. They went in a party of six of Dermot's arranging, so that for once Lord Sandiford did not make one of the number; and this circumstance caused one or two knowledgeable witnesses to enquire if he had been ousted from his position as favourite in the Martenhays matrimonial stakes. This fellow new-come from the country was a dark horse, but he seemed to be making most of the running at the moment. Came from somewhere near the Martenhays place, didn't he? Probably a friend of the family.

The rumours reached Viscount Sandiford's ears. He had already noted with strong disapproval the easy terms upon which Mr. Winfield stood with the lady. In his pursuit of Katherine he had never before acknowledged a serious rival, but now it seemed that he must do so, and just when delay might be most dangerous. He knew very well that the announcement of his betrothal to Katherine would soothe the fears of his most pressing creditors, but, with a nice calculation of the odds, he reckoned that he had no more than a month in which to bring her up to scratch. He had nothing personal against Mr. Winfield—a pleasant, unassuming sort of man if somewhat rustic in outlook—but the devil was in it that he should turn up now at such an awkward juncture of affairs.

Alarmed, he set himself to out-manoeuvre his opponent, exerting all his considerable charm, and his knowledge of the best entertainment to be found in Town, to please and amuse Katherine. He even abjured his regular attempts to redeem his fortunes at the gaming table, in favour of taking her to Almack's, that deadly dull holy of holies; and behaved so prettily, not only to Katherine herself but also to several of the Patronesses, notably Lady Jersey, that he was generally held to be reforming his way of life in preparation for entering into the bonds of matrimony. Since this was the impression that he had wished to convey, he counted the evening well spent despite its tedium. A second foray on the same front was less successful, since Mr. Winfield was also present, and Katherine danced with him twice. She danced twice with his Lordship, too, and no other gentleman was so far honoured, but that could scarcely be counted a signal victory.

His Lordship became anxious, but he could not devise any means of ridding himself of his bucolic rival. He had wild thoughts of provoking the fellow to a duel—just to incapacitate him for the necessary period. But for that to be of any use it was necessary to emerge the victor, and the fellow was reputed to be a good swordsman and a pretty fair shot with a pistol. Moreover, he was even-tempered and not addicted to heavy drinking. It would be difficult—perhaps farcical—to force a quarrel on such a man. He was well-liked, too. Sympathy would be on his side. His Lordship, unusually sensitive just now to the current of public opinion, rejected the notion. He concentrated instead on the invention of gallantries to be poured into Katherine's ears, but since she had little liking for counterfeit coin, and was very well aware that she did not outshine all other females either in point of beauty, in wit or in fashionable accomplishments, he got little good of that. She smiled and disclaimed, or even told him not to be so ridiculous. And when, driven to desperation by such cold-heartedness, he renewed his offer of marriage, she pointed out, kindly enough, that she had refused him once, and that she was not the sort of girl to change her mind. His friendship she would be sorry to lose, since she found him an agreeable companion, but she had no intention of raising unfounded hopes in his breast. Unless he could accept dismissal as final, it would be better if, in future, they avoided one another as far as possible.

He was in no position to cavil at this ultimatum. The extent to which he was seen in Miss Martenhays's company was probably the only thing that kept his creditors at bay. He would not lightly forego her society. He humbly begged pardon and promised not to transgress again.

Katherine felt guilty, as well she might. It was true that she had no intention of marrying Lord Sandiford, and she had partly salved her conscience by making that abundantly clear, but she could not help feeling that his persistent attentions were serving a very useful purpose, and that it would be rather a pity if they suddenly ceased. They seemed to exercise such a stimulating effect on Mr. Winfield. Why that gentleman was still lingering in Town she could not quite fathom. He showed no sign of taking his departure, though surely he must have a dozen urgent tasks awaiting his attention at home. She knew for a fact—he had told her so himself—that this was the first time since his salad days that he had spent the summer months in Town. Of course it was quite probably financial exigency that had driven him to rusticate so completely in the past, while this year he could afford to be a little more extravagant.

Yet somehow she did not think that the social round was any more to his taste than it was to hers. Could it possibly be—she scarcely dared to hope—that in his own casual fashion he was paying court to one Katherine Martenhays? His manner was still not in the least lover-like. He paid her no elegant compliments, sent her no posies; but when they attended the same parties he was never far from her side, and was always at hand to attend to her comfort, whether she only needed a cool drink to refresh her after an energetic country dance, or wanted her carriage summoning early because she had the headache. And she had noticed that once or twice he had deliberately filched her from under Lord Sandiford's nose. He would ask her to dance, just as his Lordship was approaching with the same intention. Once, when she had already danced with him twice, he had asked her to accompany him on a tour of their host's picture gallery. He had not suggested that Lord Sandiford go with them, though his Lordship had hovered expectantly in that hope; and they had spent an entertaining half hour in lively discussion of the portraits, Mr. Winfield displaying a vein of humour that she had not suspected in him, and offering his conjectures as to the dispositions and histories of the various subjects.

He was, in fact, delightfully attentive, but not possessive. And she wanted him to be possessive. There was no longer any doubt in her mind that she had found the man with whom she wished to spend the rest of her life, and she would not despise any shift that forwarded the possibility of a marriage between them. If Lord Sandiford's attentions made her appear more desirable to Mr. Winfield, then she would make what use she could of them.

So it came to pass that Society was treated to a comedy that entertained it delightfully. Within the week bets were being laid in the clubs as to which of the rival contestants would win the lady. A naval man, dropping in at a party where all three were present, cracked an idle jest about port and starboard watch. The idea caught on, though nobody was quite sure which of the two gentlemen was which. People would enquire with an amiable twinkle as to which watch was on duty. Through all this, the lady preserved an admirable impartiality. If she drove out with Lord Sandiford in the afternoon, she would be found riding with Mr. Winfield in the Park next morning. She might have been comforted to know that the odds on Mr. Winfield's success were shortening. He might not be wealthy, but he was a man of substance, said the knowledgeable; a man of good sense, too, with a pleasant way with him, well liked by his own sex, and quite a favourite with the ladies. If he was looking for a wife, he could take his pick of half a dozen eligible damsels. But his preference for Miss Martenhays was so marked, that the match-making mamas had resigned themselves to failure where he was concerned. If the girl could be persuaded to take Sandiford, then there might be a chance for some other maiden, but not otherwise.

Thus matters proceeded very smoothly and pleasantly, on the surface. But one of the three principals was deeply uneasy. In the early days of the rivalry Lord Sandiford had assured himself that Mr. Winfield's attachment to Katherine was a very milk and water affair, probably born of his acquaintance with her Papa—they were close neighbours, he understood—and his lack of other female acquaintance in Town. As the newcomer's circle of friends widened to include some of the real 'diamonds' of the *ton*, he would probably transfer his attentions elsewhere. After all, decided his Lordship, apart from her money there was nothing exactly intoxicating about Katherine. She was a nice little thing if you liked them quiet and pretty behaved. For himself, he preferred something a bit more dashing and colourful, though Katherine—with her dowry—would do very well as a wife. Once the knot was tied, one could always seek entertainment elsewhere. And perhaps it was better to have a wife who would be docile and submissive. After all, there was the the title to consider. That meant an heir. He would not like to think that there was any back door business when that was in question. Yes, he would content himself with the dutiful Katherine—if only he could be sure of her.

That was the rub. Mr. Winfield's courtship, if courtship it was, and not just damned interference born of friendship for the girl's father, seemed to intensify instead of dying a natural death. His Lordship had done his best to bring various other damsels to Winfield's notice. So far as he could judge, it was useless. The fellow was polite and pleasant to them, danced, chatted and returned them to their chaperones without making any attempt at improving the acquaintance. Whereas, whenever Sandiford tried to get Katherine to himself for a minute or two, he was forever falling over the fellow. What was equally alarming was his belief that Katherine liked his rival pretty well. Certainly she made no attempt to avoid his company, but rather seemed to encourage him. His Lordship's reflections grew more and more gloomy. Something would have to be done. Proposing to the girl was no good. She had said she was not the one to change her mind, and he believed her. Very well, then. She must be obliged to change it. The only problem was how to achieve this desirable result.

It took him some time to find the answer, and even longer to devise a means of accomplishing it. Not even his best friends would have described his Lordship as being fertile in invention. Moreover, he was of an easy-going disposition so long as his own comfort was not in question, and he did not really care for the notion of distressing and frightening a girl, be she never so obstinate. But after racking his brains for a couple of days, he was reluctantly forced to the conclusion that he would be obliged to compromise Katherine in order to ensure her submission to his wishes. He wouldn't really hurt her, of course, and though the resultant scandal would be unpleasant for her, it would soon be forgotten once they were safely married.

Comforting himself with such thoughts as these, he set about planning a scheme for abducting the lady and holding her captive for, perhaps, two or three days. That should be sufficient to achieve his design, and would serve the additional purpose of disposing of any objections that his prospective father-in-law might think of making to the proposed match. After such an adventure, any father would be only too thankful to have his daughter safely wed. After all, it was not as though he was just anybody. To be sure his pockets were wholly to let, but there was the title and an ancient name, and a crumbling, tumble-down ruin of a house in Sussex. Besides, he meant to be a kind husband. He would not interfere with Katherine's pleasures, so long as she was discreet, and he would see to it that she did not interfere with his. So much settled, it remained only to arrange just how the abduction should be carried out.

It should have been easy. He was sure he had heard, in a vague sort of way, of several such affairs. But it turned out to be not easy at all. He had not concerned himself particularly with the details of such cases as came to his notice, and he could scarcely seek out the principals at this late date and ask their advice on the proper conduct of an abduction. Or had they been elopements? He had an idea that Gretna Green came into it somewhere, and for that he would need a post-chaise and numerous changes of horses. And how was he to persuade the lady to go with him? She had driven with him often enough in his curricle, but a closed carriage was a very different matter. He would have to invent a very urgent errand, and explain that he had borrowed a friend's carriage in case the weather should turn wet.

All this planning and contriving was very exhausting, especially as he dared not change his usual way of life lest any one grow suspicious. His manner grew more and more abstracted as he wrestled mentally with the awkward problems that kept presenting themselves to his imagination. Katherine, ascribing his lack of spirits to anxiety over financial matters, felt quite sorry for him, and did her best to distract his thoughts, accepting his suggestions for various outings in an uncritical spirit, and feigning an enjoyment that she did not really feel.

It took him a full week to complete his plans. They were complicated by his determination to manage the whole thing himself, with only the help of his groom. To be bringing strangers into such a business was both distasteful and dangerous. Besides they would have to be heavily bribed, and he simply did not have the money. For the same reason a post-chaise was out of the question. Postilions were notorious gabblemongers, unless they were handsomely greased in the fist. A neat, light chaise, with his own groom to drive it. That was the ticket. And he had thought of an unexceptionable pretext for the outing. He would take Katherine to make the acquaintance of his Cousin Charlotte. She lived in Kensington, and was married to an officer in the Guards. So much was perfectly true. The fact that she was at present in Leicestershire at her parents' home, awaiting the birth of her first child, need not emerge. He could tell a pitiful tale of her loneliness, say she was just new come to Town, and longed for congenial feminine company. That ought to turn the trick with the tender-hearted Katherine, and persuade her to overlook the impropriety of driving alone with him in a chaise.

Once he had her safely installed in the chaise, the rest was comparatively simple. Jason would have orders to drive them straight to the Grey Goose Feathers, a snug little hostelry just off the Great North Road. Its landlord, an ex-prize-fighter, had a kindness for his Lordship, who had been one of his patrons during his fighting career. He could be trusted to turn a deaf ear to pleas for help. And his sister, a tight-lipped Amazon, would supply such woman's gear as Katherine would require for her brief stay. No doubt it would be pretty rough, not at all what she was accustomed to, but she should be thankful for even such simple provision for her comfort. He himself had no intention of laying a finger on her. Her absence from home, her presence alone with him, unchaperoned, would be quite sufficient to enforce her consent to his proposal. No one would ever believe that her sojourn in the inn had been wholly innocent.

TEN

It seemed that, for once, fortune had decided to smile upon his endeavours, for his plans worked more smoothly than he had expected. Katherine lent a sympathetic ear to the tale of his cousin's predicament, and promised to go with him to call upon her. Tippy Warner was perfectly willing to lend his light town chaise, giving only half an ear to his Lordship's tale of escorting Miss Martenhays to visit friends, and never thinking of enquiring as to why the lady could not use her own perfectly adequate carriage. To be sure, Katherine looked rather doubtful when he presented himself with a chaise instead of the curricle that she was expecting, but the sky was rather overcast which might well presage

rain, so his Lordship's explanation about the
desirability of a closed carriage sounded plau-
sible enough. She did consider summoning an
abigail to go with her, but, as it chanced, she
had sent her own maid on an errand from which
she was not yet returned. She decided that she
was being unnecessarily fussy over so short a
journey, and mounted into the chaise without
further hesitation.

Lord Sandiford then proceeded to regale her
with a long and detailed account of his friendship with Mr. Warner, the owner of the elegant
chaise in which she was riding. It began with
the two of them at school together, and it was
exceedingly dull, but good manners compelled
her to attend to it, and even to ask one or two
helpful questions which set the narrator off
again. She did not for a moment suspect that
they were not bound for Kensington, but were
working their way steadily northward.

She did think, however, that they must be
taking a roundabout route. Not only did the
journey seem unduly protracted—which might
have been the effect of his Lordship's saga—but
she saw no recognisable landmarks. However,
this was easily explained. When she enquired,
she was told that his Lordship had wished to
try out the carriage a bit, because his cousins
were thinking of buying it from Tippy. He was
duly apologetic for the delay, but did Katherine
not think that the vehicle was extremely com-

fortable? He was discovering in himself an ingenuity in answering awkward questions that filled him with admiration.

But even he could not explain away the Red Lion in Barnet, or convince Katherine that it stood within the purlieus of Kensington. The inn was far too familiar, since she and Papa always changed horses there on their way north.

She sprang erect in her seat with a startled exclamation. Lord Sandiford leaned forward and rapped sharply on the panel behind the driver, at which pre-arranged signal Jason obeyed his orders to, "Spring 'em."

The bays had been carefully nursed over the initial stages of the journey. They were still full of fire and energy, and flung themselves into their collars with hearty good will. Mr. Warner's chaise, for its class, was lightly built. It bounded over the road at what seemed to Katherine a terrifying speed. She was obliged to hold very tightly with both hands to keep herself safe in her seat. And the noise of hooves and wheels pounding over the road made conversation impossible. But she was not seriously alarmed. If this was one of Master Julian's pranks, she would give him a rare trimming as soon as she had the opportunity.

In the small yard that served the Grey Goose Feathers, she came down from the carriage in very dignified fashion, disdaining his Lordship's proffered hand; a slim, resolute little creature whom he found oddly daunting, despite her physical frailty. Since the inn did not boast a private parlour—and since, in any case, she did not think that she wanted to be closeted in a private room with Sandiford—she consented to being ushered into the coffee room; though she declined all offers of refreshment, thereby obliging his Lordship, who felt that, after the mental strain of the past hour he stood sorely in need of the reviving qualities of a tankard of home-brewed, to follow her example.

She also refused to sit down, standing very straight and composed in front of the empty hearth, and sternly demanding an explanation of his behaviour.

"And don't try to cozen me with any more Banbury tales about your cousin," she finished severely. "I begin to doubt the very existence of this cousin. Just tell me in round terms what sort of a rig you are running this time. Is it some wager?"

Instead of immediately asserting his masculine authority, and terrifying this insubordinate chit into submission, the unfortunate Viscount found himself entangled in a sea of half phrases of assurance that he really did have a Cousin Charlotte, and that his peculiar actions were not directed towards the winning of a wager. Nor was he running any sort of a rig.

"The truth of the matter is, ma'am," he

snorted suddenly, realising that his apologetic protestations were only weakening his position, "that I've abducted you."

That did startle her. But she could not really be afraid of Julian, and she made a quick recovery. "Nonsense," she said stoutly, though she was aware of a certain inward quaking. "You would not do anything so unkind. Or only by way of some stupid jest," she excused him, trying to sound braver than she felt.

He assured her that it was no jest. "You would not marry me when I offered for you fairly," he said sullenly. "Now I will leave you no choice. A couple of days hid away here, and you must marry me, or be utterly disgraced and cast out by Society."

She eyed him steadily, and decided that he meant what he said. An ugly scowl disfigured his good-looking face, and his jaw was thrust out in very determined fashion. She said slowly, "You have surprised me, milord."

His militant pose relaxed. She was going to surrender! "I have?"

"Yes. I never thought to find you cow-hearted."

He flushed with fury at the insult. "No one has ever said that of me and gone scot free," he said stiffly.

"But I do. I say it," she told him tranquilly. "Just because I have no brother or cousin to defend me, you think that you can entreat me as you will. If I had a champion to fight my

battles for me it would be a different story. Let
me assure you, milord, that I will never consent
to marry you. You may drag my name through
the mud of your despicable plot, but yours will
be the infamy. Not only cow-hearted but a liar
and treacherous too. I am well rid of you."

"Valiant words, my dear," retorted his Lordship angrily. "But you are not yet rid of me.
Better think of that before you flay me further
with that waspish tongue of yours. It seems to
me that a period of quiet reflection on your situation might be of benefit. You will retire to
the chamber that has been prepared for you,
and we shall see if solitude and the knowledge
that you can entertain no hope of rescue, do not
bring you to a more amenable frame of mind.
No need yet to resort to stronger measures. Your
meals will be served to you in your room. The
window is securely shuttered and the shutters
barred. Nor will bribery avail you. Matilda who
will wait on you is quite devoted to my interests.
Better resign yourself. I regret that there are
no books or other means of beguiling the tedium
of your imprisonment. You must amuse yourself
by planning your honeymoon."

He could not resist that last jibe, for her fierce
defiance had flicked him on the raw. There was
a good deal of decency in him still. Only desperation had driven him to behave so ill to one
who had never shown him anything but friendship. Treacherous, too, whispered a small inner

voice. He shook his head fiercely, and locked the prison door. He did not bother to remove the key from the lock. There was only one key and Matilda would need it when she came to wait on the prisoner. With the bird safely caged he felt secure enough, and that last cut about the honeymoon had, a little, revived his self esteem. After all, it was not as though he planned to rape the girl. All he wanted was to marry her. If she continued obdurate, he supposed it might after all be necessary to proceed to Gretna Green, and wondered if Katherine had enough money about her to pay for the expense of such a journey. It was no use asking Samson, who would trust him with anything but money.

Samson, however, had at least a suggestion for enlivening the long hours of an evening spent at the Grey Goose Feathers. In fact, he offered a double bill. At an inn slightly more remote from the eye of the law, a cock fight was to be staged. Just a few peaceable country gentlemen, each assured that his bird was the best, and willing to stake a little blunt to back his opinion. And if that did not provide suffi-cient entertainment, there was to be an exhi-bition match between a local middle weight of considerable promise and a protegé of Sir Joshua's brought up from London. Sir Joshua— the Squire—was a patron of the Fancy. It would be interesting to see how the youngsters showed up.

Lord Sandiford was well pleased. His entertainment for the evening was assured. He might even win a guinea or two by judicious staking against these country bumpkins who were so pleased with the birds of their own breeding. The thought of his captive gave him no concern. No slip of a girl, locked into a shuttered room, even if it was on the ground floor was going to give Matilda the bag. Matilda would make two of her—could handle her with one hand tied behind her. Besides, it would be just as well to leave the headstrong chit severely alone. Tomorrow would be time enough to deal with her tears and recriminations.

Katherine's heart sank at the first sight of her wardress. She had never seen so masculine a woman. She was massively built without being fat and there was no hint of feminine softness about the craggy features or the muscular limbs. Nor was there anything yielding in voice or attitude. To Katherine's tentative enquiry as to how she should address her, she barked out, "Ye can call me 'Tilda. Ye don't need to know no more than that."

At least she was not actively unkind. She supplied her prisoner with the means of making a simple toilet, and with a voluminous bed gown that would have enveloped her three times over; and the food that she served was well prepared and savoury, though Katherine had little appetite for it. As his Lordship had all too truly prophesied, solitude and helplessness were already exercising their depressing effect on her spirits. The spurt of defiance with which she had outfaced her captor had died. She was not completely cowed, because she still could not be really frightened of Julian. Somehow he was not the stuff of which thorough-going villains were made. But she was miserably anxious, and, try as she would, she could see no way out of the impasse. When her jailer came to remove the supper dishes, she thanked her politely and praised the cooking, apologising that she had eaten so little. She thought she detected the faintest softening in the granite countenance, and chanced another enquiry. After all, the woman was her only link with the outside world.

"You will understand that I feel too anxious to eat," she explained, with a brave attempt at a smile. "And do tell me, why is it so quiet? This is an inn, is it not? Yet there is no sound of roistering or revelry. All is silent. It is very strange and rather frightening."

Perhaps Matilda had been touched by the compliment to her cooking. Perhaps her professional pride was stung by the suggestion that the Grey Goose Feathers was ill patronised. She said gruffly, "You're at the back of the house. Tap's at the front, so you don't 'ear the men so plain. Any way there's not so many in tonight. Some fight—fisticuffs—they've all gone off to see. But I've better things to do than to stand 'ere gabbing. Get thee between sheets, and may a night's sleep send thee good sense, so that thou takes up no more of a busy woman's time."

There was nothing more to be got from her, and presently, since there was nothing else to do, Katherine took her advice and climbed into bed.

ELEVEN

Dermot had not intended to call on Lady Julia and her charge on that fateful afternoon. He had not yet reached a decision as to what he was to do about his love for Katherine, and, from time to time, he strove to subdue it by avoiding her presence for a little while. Then anxiety as to the progress that Lord Sandiford might be making in his absence, or just his own natural longing to be with her as much as possible, would draw him back again. He was in something of a quandary. His reason for coming to Town had been primarily the urge to protect Miss Martenhays from the machinations of a fortune-hunter. At least, he thought it had. But so far as he could judge, the lady was well able to look after herself. He had seen her cool reception of some of his Lordship's more exaggerated flights, the amused little smile with which she fended off his possessive airs. It appeared that this particular suitor was making no headway.

Yet he could not bring himself to abandoning Katherine to conduct her life in her own way. That was pure selfishness of course. He knew exactly what he wanted her to do, but so far, he had restrained himself from actual lovemaking. It was her wretched fortune that stuck in his gullet. If he paid court to her—as he so longed to do—she, and all the other interested parties, of whom there were far too many, would think it was only cupboard love. He knew that he should not permit such considerations to affect his judgement, but the thought rankled. Perhaps he was being ridiculously prickly, for he could offer Katherine a comfortable establishment and an income sufficient to support a genteel way of life. But there would be no margin for such luxuries as jewels and a Town house, a smart carriage and fine horses. The fact that Katherine had shown no particular liking for such things had no bearing on the case. He wanted to bestow them upon her. If her father's money provided them it was not the same thing at all.

He was still seeking a solution to this knotty problem when an old friend of his mother's

offered him the use of her box at the Opera.
So far as he knew, neither Lady Julia nor
Katherine was particularly musically inclined,
or no more so than was necessary to give the
right social impression. He knew that Katherine played the pianoforte quite prettily, but
she had never gone into raptures over the per-
formance of the latest fashionable singer. However, a box at the Opera offered rather more
than a musical treat. It was a great occasion.
The ladies wore their finest toilets and as many
jewels as good taste permitted. In the intervals
they recieved all the friends who had noted
their exalted position. He must not allow his
own uncertainties to deny Katherine this unexpected treat.

He found Lady Julia yawning over a fashion
magazine, very happy to receive a visitor, and
delighted with the invitation that he brought.
They had no important engagement for that
evening and she was sure that Katherine would
be as pleased as she was. Her only doubt was
whether the girl would be back from her afternoon visit in time to make the elaborate toilet
that should grace such an occasion. Katherine's
maid, called into consultation, could offer no
precise information as to the time when her
mistress might be expected to return.

"In fact I wondered if she'd changed her
plans, milady, seeing as Simmons tells me she
went off with Lord Sandiford in a chaise."

Lady Julia looked startled. "In a chaise?" she repeated. "Are you sure?"

"I didn't see her myself, milady," returned the handmaiden, who had been dying to canvas this unusual piece of behaviour ever since it had been reported to her, "but that's what Simmons said. A chaise and pair. His Lordship's own bays with his groom driving."

This detailed account drew Lady Julia's attention to the girl's excessive interest. Her first reaction of mild dismay deepened. Even the servants saw Katherine's behaviour as strange. And it never paid to set servants gossiping.

"Very well, Essie," she said dismissively. "Ask Simmons to come up to the parlour if it is convenient."

Lady Julia's modest establishment did not boast a butler. Indoor men servants, she had been heard to declare, were more trouble than they were worth. Envious friends were wont to retort that such an attitude was all very well when you had a Simmons to fill all the awkward gaps in domestic comfort. Simmons had spent all his working years in good service. When he married Lady Julia's excellent cook he saw no reason to change his way of life. He would just extend his field of operations. A good-humoured fellow, with no exaggerated idea of his own importance, he was willing to turn his hand to anything. He played footman at Lady Julia's parties, acted as intermediary between her and

the owner of the livery stable that she patronised when in Town, and was not above moving
heavy furniture, taking up carpets or performing such tasks as he felt required masculine
strength. He and his wife lived very snugly in
a little house in the old mews, and when teased
by her friends about the way she indulged the
pair of them, Lady Julia retorted that such treasures deserved every indulgence that she could
contrive. The only small drawback lay in the
fact that you never knew what Simmons might
be doing at any given moment. If he was cleaning silver or polishing glasses he would not
mind being disturbed. If he was decanting wine
there might be some delay.

On this occasion he responded to Lady Julia's summons with commendable promptitude.
Possibly he had been expecting it. But he could
add little to the information that Essie had
already provided. On one point, however, he
was very helpful. To Mr. Winfield's enquiries
about the chaise, he furnished a brief description.

"No, sir. Not hired. An ugly colour—at least
to my mind—a sort of light tan. But everything
of the first stare. Double steps, silver plating
wherever there was room for it, a barouche driving seat, and green silk curtains trimmed with
orange and white fringe. I noticed those particularly because his Lordship let them fall across

the window as soon as he had handed Miss Katherine in."

"I don't like it," said Lady Julia uneasily, when Simmons had taken his departure. "Why a chaise if she was only going to visit a cousin in Kensington? And if any word had come from her Papa that necessitated her travelling further afield, she would have left a message for me, and would have taken her maid with her. Surely that wretched young man cannot have persuaded her to elope with him? She is fond of him, but only as one likes a pet dog, I swear it. She's not in love with him. In any case, even if she is, why elope? She is of age, and may marry where she chooses; although naturally it will be an object with her to win her father's consent."

"It doesn't sound like an elopement," suggested Dermot soothingly. "There was no mention of baggage, which would surely be essential in such a case. But I confess I am a little uneasy. How would it be if I were to make a few enquiries and see if I can hit upon the route they took? If Simmons's description is to be believed, some one is bound to have noticed that chaise."

Lady Julia approving the suggestion, he went off to put it into practice, asking her to send word to Fenton's if Katherine were to return in the meanwhile.

Though he had spoken reassuringly to Lady

Julia, he was deeply concerned. He did not think for one moment that Katherine had eloped, but he had heard the rumours about Lord Sandiford's financial difficulties, and he could not rule out the possibility that the fellow had used some trick to carry her off in an attempt to force her into marriage. It was this possibility, far-fetched as it seemed, that he was so anxious to investigate. If the missing pair had gone off on some innocent pleasure excursion, Katherine would return in her own good time. If she had been forcibly abducted it was a very different matter.

He went round to the livery stables to order the hack that he had ridden on several occasions since coming to Town, and was so fortunate as to find it not only available but fit and fresh. While he changed swiftly into riding clothes, he planned a circuit which would cover the main roads out of Town. If Sandiford was planning a journey of any distance he would have to change horses. The posting houses were the obvious places to initiate enquiries.

Three times he drew blank, and it might have proved a long and exhausting task had not Lord Sandiford overlooked one or two of the finer points of planning an abduction. He would have done better to use an unobtrusive vehicle rather than Mr. Warner's elegant but highly noticeable chaise; and better still to hire horses rather than use his own famous bays. True, they had not stopped at the Red Lion, but the ostlers there, always on the watch for likely customers, remembered the chaise as soon as Dermot described it. They had not seen his Lordship but they had recognised his horses and his groom. They were even able to say which road he had taken, for the speed at which the chaise had left Barnet had focused attention on it. "Set off as if the devil 'isself was on 'is 'eels," volunteered one witness.

But after Barnet Mr. Winfield suffered a check. No one in Potters Bar had noticed the tan-coloured chaise, yet surely Sandiford, not the sort of man to outface his cattle, could not intend to push on as far as Hatfield? Those bays must already be hanging on his hands. If he had taken to the side roads he might be planning to rack up somewhere for the night; and it could be anywhere, though it was likely to be a small place, and quiet. If, as Dermot surmised, he was hoping to force Katherine into marriage, he would not want any actual scandal, though he would hold the threat of it over the girl's head. He decided that his best chance was to cast back and investigate any promising side roads and small hostelries. It was an infuriating task, and he was beginning to think it a hopeless one when sheer chance led him to the Grey Goose Feathers. He had given it one swift assessing glance and had almost ridden past. It was too small for San-

diford's purpose, he reckoned, and seemed to
be deserted. The shutters were already up
across one window, and that was unusual with
still an hour of daylight left. Perhaps it was
that shuttered window that invited him to sur-
vey the place more closely. He rode round to
the front, and there, drawn to one side, was
the chaise he was seeking. It had been wheeled
out of a large, barn-like building which served
the inn as stable and coach house combined,
and its elegance looked sadly out of place in
those shabby surroundings. A few scrawny
hens were scratching despondently in the dusty
yard, and there was a strong aroma of pig. A
thin slip of a lad, whom Dermot judged to be
about twelve or thirteen years of age, was so
engrossed in restoring the glossy panels to
their pristine perfection that he remained unaware of the newcomer's approach until Dermot addressed him.

He glanced up from his task, eyes widening
in amazement at the realisation that two proper
swells should have chosen to honour the Grey
Goose Feathers on one and the same day. But
he was an intelligent youth despite his rustic
appearance, and it soon occurred to him that
this gentry cove had perhaps come in search of
the other one.

"Wos you looking for Lord Sandiford, sir?"
he enquired eagerly. "Bloke as owns this chaise?
A 'cause I'm sorry to say 'e's not 'ere. 'E's gorn

orf wiv Mister Keane—the landlord—to watch
some cock-fighting. And some fisticuffs, too,"
he added on a wistful note. Cock-fighting did
not much appeal to him, but he would dearly
have loved to see that turn-up; though there
was some degree of pleasure to be got from
handling a bang-up turn-out like this one.

Dermot, thanking him heartily, if silently,
for his unsolicited help, asked if he could be
accommodated for the night. The boy was doubtful.

"Best ask the missis," he decided. "'S' only a
small place and some of the rooms already
taken. Shall I 'old your 'orse, sir, while you goes
to talk to 'er? Round that way. She'll be in the
kitchen."

Thus directed, Dermot made his way round to
the kitchen quarters and made the acquaintance
of Miss Matilda Keane. No, she said, she was
sorry to be disobliging but her rooms were already taken. She had only the two. The groom's
quarters were quite unsuitable for a gentleman.
He had best ride on to North Mimms or Water
End. Dermot accepted this in good part, feeling
that he was on a hot scent with his quarry almost
in view. He thought again about that shuttered
window. There could be an excellent reason for
it. And unless he was much mistaken, that kind
of shutter opened easily enough from the outside,
provided one could force the lock without undue
noise. He explained to Miss Keane that both he

and his horse were in need of rest and refreshment before embarking on a further search for accommodation. The lady would have liked to refuse, but felt that to do so would arouse suspicion.

She said grumpily that Tom would see to his horse, but that he himself must make do with plain fare. "We don't reckon to cater for the gentry, but if you're sharp-set there's ham and eggs or the end of a cold mutton pie."

Mr. Winfield, accepting this Spartan fare with admirable tolerance, was presently ushered into the inn's diminutive coffee room. He sat down to his simple meal with renewed confidence. While overlooking the provision for his horse, he had chanced to see Lord Sandiford's bays. His Lordship, one of whose more endearing qualities was a total lack of regard for his own consequence, had driven off quite contentedly to his evening's entertainment in the landlord's gig. His bays, as Dermot had suspected, had done more than enough. The sight of them bedded down as comfortably as was possible in the rather rough and ready conditions prevailing at the inn was a powerful stimulant to Dermot's conviction that somehow he must have Katherine away out of this perilous situation. He was not quite sure how it was to be managed. His own mount was pretty weary, but could be relied upon to carry Katherine's light weight for a few miles yet, and those bays were in no case to set out in pursuit. Not that he thought there would be any pursuit. Let him but get the girl safely away before Sandiford returned, and he rather thought that milord would concede defeat.

The next thing to be done was to establish communication with the prisoner, for prisoner he was convinced that she was. Finishing his meal he pondered the problem of how to distract Miss Keane's attention while he investigated that shuttered room. The coffee room was next door to the tap, and having served his meal she had gone back to her duties there. Since a glance through the open door had shown him that there were no more than half a dozen customers, the duties were not very onerous, and he could not rely upon them to keep her fully occupied. He strolled into the tap and asked if she could make him a bowl of rum punch, complimenting her on the excellence of the mutton pie. There was no softening in her manner despite his pleasant address.

"It'll take me nigh on half an hour," she told him sourly, "what with the fire burnt low and the kettle to boil, not to mention the lemon to squeeze and nutmeg to grate and me single-handed tonight. By that time it'll be full dark and your honour still with a bed to seek. Ye'd do better to ride on to North Mimms, like I said."

Dermot assured her cheerfully that he had no

objection to the delay, watched her dispense a couple of mugs of ale to her thirsty customers, and saw her started safely kitchenward before he returned to the coffee room. Thence he moved swiftly enough.

The shuttered room lay at the back of the house, almost opposite the coffee room, and he had taken care to close the tap-room door behind him. Two swift strides took him to the locked door. To his amazement the key was in the lock. He did not hesitate but turned it and opened the door a crack, exclaiming urgently, "Katherine! Are you there? It's Dermot Winfield."

An anxious mind and a lumpy mattress are not conducive to peaceful slumber. Katherine had been tossing restlessly, striving in vain to find some way out of her dilemma that would save her from a forced marriage. The sound of the key turning in the lock brought her wide awake, sitting up in bed with the covers clutched to her breast, her heart thumping wildly at the invasion of her privacy.

The unexpected prospect of escape suggested by Dermot's softly spoken words caused her to forget all about the behaviour proper to a young lady surprised in her bed by a visit from a gentleman.

"How did you find me? Oh! Thank God that you did," she said breathlessly, instinctively keeping her voice low. "You'll help me out of this coil, won't you? I swear I hadn't the least notion of what he meant to do. Oh! Please take me back to Aunt Julia."

"Precisely what I have in mind, child, so stop fretting," returned the soft, confident whisper. She could just make out the loom of his tall figure against the streak of dim light admitted by the partly opened door, and spared a moment to hope that he could not see her. "But it will not do to run away without a proper plan of escape. We have only one tired nag between us until we reach the next posting inn—some four or five miles. It won't do to raise a hue and cry on our tails. With your permission I'll leave you, briefly, or the landlady will be looking for me. Give me half an hour and I'll be tapping on your window. Can you be ready to come with me then, as quietly as possible? My whole idea is to snatch you away leaving no one the wiser until we're out of reach of pursuit."

Yes, she could be ready. Somehow she would make shift to dress in the dark. Her appearance did not matter. All that counted was to win free of this stuffy chamber and his Lordship's odious plans. She even smiled as she heard the key turn in the lock once more. Her fellow conspirator was taking no risks. She climbed out of bed and began to feel round about for her clothes.

TWELVE

Mr. Winfield was lounging indolently over the table in the coffee room when Miss Keane brought in her aromatic offering, and dumped it unceremoniously beside him. She was terse and tetchy.

"Will that be all, sir? Because I've my other customers in the tap to attend to."

Dermot assured her that he had no further requirements and said that he would settle his reckoning there and then in order to spare her the trouble of another interruption in her duties. She had the grace to look a little shamefaced, but when he said that he would like his horse in half an hour's time she told him gruffly that he would have to saddle up for himself.

"We've but the one ostler," she explained, "and he's gone off with my brother. Tom, the stable boy, is only a lad that comes in to help. His mother likes him home before the darkening. The lantern's lit in the stable. You'll manage well enough."

Nothing could have suited him better, but he made that pretence of annoyance that he knew she would expect, mumbling something under his breath that might be taken as a reflection on the standard of hospitality prevailing at the Grey Goose Feathers. This took very well, the lady thawing into something that was almost geniality, as she informed him that he had come on a bad day, and that one woman could not be expected to attend to the tap room and the stables and house guests as well, but that if he chose to call in again on his return journey and found her better placed, she would show him what she could do in the way of a neat plain dinner.

They parted, each with a certain degree of respect for the other, she to return to her taproom responsibilities, he to make pretence of sipping his rum punch while he considered the details of his plan for freeing Katherine. It did not take him long to decide that the sooner it was put into operation the better. It might not be so very long before Lord Sandiford, the landlord and the ostler returned to augment the forces arrayed against him. Best if he and Katherine could be away before that happened. He pondered the disposal of a bowl of rum punch. Having made such a point of ordering it, it would be highly suspicious to depart leaving it to cool on the table, but this was no time to be getting top-heavy from injudicious potations. There was no suitable receptacle in the coffee room, no convenient vase or bowl of flowers. Cautiously he tried the casement window. It opened sweetly enough at a gentle touch, giving him a much better appreciation of Miss Keane's housekeeping. He leaned out quietly, peering into the gathering darkness. He could detect no sign of life, save for a climbing rose that encircled the window and startled him by catching at his sleeve. Gently he poured a libation of rum about its thorny feet and hoped it was duly appreciative. That done, he gathered up hat and whip and took his departure, putting his head round the tap-room door to bid Miss Keane good night, assuring her that he would be off now and thanking her politely for her hospitality. The gesture was quite unnecessary, the thanks certainly unjustified, but he hoped that his behaviour would dispel any lingering suspicions that Miss Keane might be nourishing about his reason for visiting the Grey Goose Feathers, and so make it possible for Katherine and him to show a clean pair of heels to any possible pursuit. He then betook himself to the stables, where he saddled his horse and presently trotted down the lane that led towards the Great North Road, keeping his eyes open for a likely place to secure the nag while he himself returned for Katherine. A farm gate, set a little back from the road, looked inviting. He opened it and led his horse through into a small copse which seemed ideal for his purpose. Even when the moon rose it seemed unlikely that any one would notice that there was a horse tucked away among the sapling trees. Nevertheless, he penetrated as far as possible into the copse before he secured the horse and made his way swiftly back to the inn.

All was still quiet. He circled it watchfully. The stable lantern still glowed, as did the lights in the entry and tap-room. There was a subdued hum of talk audible as he passed the tap-room window, but otherwise all was quiet. Certainly there was no sound of an approaching vehicle which might spell disaster to his plans. Treading swiftly, now, but softly, he moved round to the back of the inn and to the shuttered window. It was very dark, for the moon had barely reached the half and this side of the building lay in shadow. He explored the shutters carefully with his finger tips and sighed his relief. No padlock. Just a heavy iron bar fastened with a button, the shutters themselves warped by the weather. He had to lean the whole of his weight against them before he could persuade the button to turn, but he managed it with only the smallest squeak from the protesting iron. It was rather more awkward to lift the bar down, until he discovered that it was hinged at one end. The shutters needed coaxing, the right hand one having to be lifted down first, whereupon its brother followed easily enough. He laid them flat on their faces in the yard where they could not trip his feet, and returned to the window. Katherine had already pushed the casement wide, for although he had made very little noise she had been listening eagerly for his coming. He set his hands about her waist and lifted her over the low sill, carefully pushing the casement to, so that it would not attract attention. Then he picked her up bodily, laying her across his shoulder and bidding her hold tight as he made for the yard gate, keeping to the deepest shadow as far as possible and hoping that none of the drinkers would choose this moment to set out for home. Not that his comings and goings were any concern of theirs, but he did not wish to leave any witness who could say which way he had gone. He had skirted the stable with its betraying glow of light, and had almost reached the gate when he heard the inn door open. He carried his burden through the gate and dragged it shut behind him, set Katherine on her feet and took her hand in a firm clasp. "Run for it," he ordered briskly. "Not far to where I left the horse, and let's hope those fellows are going the other way."

They ran, Katherine stumbling over the rough surface of the lane in her thin slippers, but steadied by the strong hand that held her from falling. She managed a little better as her eyes became accustomed to the gloom, but was thankful enough when Dermot called a halt at the gate that opened on to the copse. She clung to the top bar thankfully, trying to still her hurried breathing, as she saw that his head was tilted back the way they had come, listening for sounds of pursuit.

All was quiet. Whoever had left the inn as they were making their own escape must have turned the other way on reaching the lane. Dermot brought the horse and lifted Katherine on to the saddle. He teased her a little, ascribing her silence to fear of re-capture, and doing his best to laugh her out of it, reminding her of the last occasion on which he had been obliged to perform this service for her, and warning her, in a very solemn voice, that she really must not make a habit of this tendency to claim his services as knight errant. He fancied he saw the flicker of a smile break the tension of her still little face, but it was too dark to be sure and he concentrated his attention on encouraging his weary mount.

The going was a little easier when they reached the post road, though now they had to face the hazard of meeting other travellers. There was the risk that Lord Sandiford would be among them, and not even a Good Samaritan stranger would be welcome in their present circumstances. Until they could reach some inn where they could hire a vehicle to convey them the rest of the way, Dermot had no desire for contact with his fellows, however kindly intentioned. The natural tendency of passing vehicles to slow down slightly as they overtook the plodding pair gave him one or two bad moments, and he was thankful indeed to see the welcoming lights of a small posting inn.

With only one horse between them and that one saddled for a gentleman, no servants and no luggage, they aroused a strong degree of curiosity in the ostler who came forward to enquire as to their needs. He stared at them with bulging eyes. But Dermot's air of quiet assurance, and the size of the roll of bank notes that he pulled out of the inner pocket of his coat, brought satisfactory results. The man swallowed his curiosity and served them deferentially. A post-chaise and four was figged out—a good even team, declared the ostler. The weary animal that had served them so well should be cared for and returned to its own stable tomorrow. The postilion mounted to his place, Dermot handed Katherine into the chaise and climbed in beside her, and the vehicle pulled out of the yard and took the

London road. Dermot gave a great sigh of relief for the accomplishment of the most vital part of his mission.

Katherine was very quiet. She had thanked him when he handed her up into the carriage, and had pressed his hand so convulsively as she did so that he had understood her thanks to extend to far more than gratitude for so simple a courtesy, but once seated she had relapsed into silence. Her thoughts could scarcely be pleasant, he guessed. Though she had been delivered from her prison, her situation was still an uncomfortable one and would provoke a good deal of unkind comment in the polite world should its history ever become known. He began to assure her that she could perfectly rely upon him. It would not be so very late when she reached home. Perhaps no more than two o'clock. She must often have been as late as that in returning from a party. Lady Julia would be so pleased to see her safe and sound that she would not be cross, and, for his part, he would never breathe a word to a soul about the evening's events.

She gave an odd little laugh and said quietly, "No need to tell me that, I could not even imagine you as a mischiefmaker. Nor would you ever have tried to coerce me against my will. Not that Sandiford would have succeeded, as I told him. I can never be sufficiently grateful to you for coming to my rescue—and I want to hear the full tale of how that came about—but even if you had not, I would never have yielded. He thought to frighten me with threats that I would lose my reputation, and so would be obliged to marry him, but I would never have consented. Better to accept the snubs and humiliations of Society, better indeed to retire from the social scene than to endure a life-time of misery tied to a man who only wants me for my father's money. And my father would have been the first to supoort me in that decision."

All very much as he had suspected. But hearing it put into blunt words by the gentle girl who had suffered such insult only released his anger. He regretted that for Katherine's own sake it had been necessary to remove her from the scene with the least possible noise. A reckoning with Sandiford would have been very much to his taste. He must see how it could be contrived. But that would keep until he had restored Katherine to the shelter of her aunt's home.

He said equably, "I trust that there is little harm done. In half an hour's time you will be safe at home. So far as I can see there is no one to tattle. For his own pride's sake, Sandiford will not speak, and since you can perfectly rely upon your father's support I would advise you to tell him the whole. Should there

be any rumours—though I cannot suppose it—
he will know very well how to deal with them."

"I shall certainly confide in Papa," agreed
Katherine, and managed a rather uncertain
chuckle. "He will probably tell me that I got my
just deserts for being too naive and trusting; but
as you say, he will undoubtedly know how to
look after me."

And so would I, thought Dermot fiercely. He
longed to take her in his arms, not in a burst
of furious acquisitive passion, but gently, pro-
tectively, as became her weary body and strained
nerves. He would woo her so gently, so tenderly
that she would draw new strength from his firm
clasp. But it was impossible. If he made her an
offer here and now she was sure to think that
it was prompted by some chivalrous notion of
suggesting a way out of her difficulties. Worse
still, she might feel herself under an obligation
to accept out of gratitude because he had just
rendered her a signal service.

He spoke instead of various impersonal topics, teasing her gently about the operatic treat
that she had missed by being out of Town that
night, until her increasingly stilted replies
advised him that reaction had her in its grip,
and he judged it better to relapse into silence.

It was two o'clock before he was able to re-
linquish an exhausted girl into the care of Lady
Julia. That lady's deep thankfulness expressed
itself in an initial burst of scolding, but Dermot

noticed with some amusement that this actually seemed to exert a soothing effect upon its recipient. She begged pardon very sincerely for having given her guardian cause for concern, protested that it was not entirely her own fault, and accepted the offer of a glass of hot milk to invite sound sleep. He had nothing to do but make his farewells and repair to his hotel, mulling over the best way of bringing Lord Sandiford to book for his dastardly conduct.

THIRTEEN

He paid a morning call on the ladies next day, but only Lady Julia recieved him. She had insisted, she explained, that Katherine take breakfast in bed, and stay there for the rest of the morning.

"The foolish child was bent on doing a number of imprudent things," she told him. "Said that she would ride in the Park, just as usual, and do a little shopping afterwards. Announced that after all you had done for her she felt that it behoved her to present the appearance of normality, so that no one should have cause to suspect her unpleasant adventure. I managed to convince her that it was perfectly normal to spend a morning in idleness, especially so late

177

in the Season and the weather so sultry. She begged me to try to thank you adequately for your help yesterday, but it is a task quite beyond my powers, for myself as well as for Katherine. If you had not found her and brought her back to me she would have been utterly ruined. And it's no good talking wildly, as I'm afraid she did about defying public opinion. She would have been obliged to marry the wretch. You have saved her from a life-time of regret, and I do not wonder at it that she does not know how to express her sense of obligation."

A much embarrassed Dermot assured her that it was a privilege to have been of service to his friends, and embarked on a half humourous account of the various chances that had favoured his search. "The veriest blunderer," he assured her, "but the luck was on my side." He made no mention of his determination to have a reckoning with Lord Sandiford. That was a matter of some delicacy. His heart was wholly set on it, but it must be so arranged that Katherine was in no way involved. He came reluctantly to the conclusion that it would not do to call the fellow out. That would be bound to arouse curiosity and speculation, and knowing the degree of attention that his Lordship had bestowed on the girl, it was extremely probable that the gossips would come very near the truth. But he could see no reason why he should not give the impudent knave a sound thrashing.

In fact, in some respects it would be more satisfactory, since he was filled with a primitive desire to smash his fists into that aristocratic face. Perhaps that wouldn't serve either, he reflected ruefully. Wouldn't do to mark him too much. Still, it should be possible to inflict a satisfactory punishment even with that restriction.

With this amiable intention in mind, he went off to Lord Sandiford's lodging. This was a pleasant apartment in the house of a retired gentleman's gentleman, who augmented his modest income by letting the larger part of his house to selected bachelor tenants. The poor misguided man had thought that to include a peer among them would add a certain distinction to his establishment, but he had very soon discovered his error. What with waiting weeks at a time for his rent, and fending off bailiffs and debt collectors who were always at his Lordship's heels, Mr. Todmore had just about come to the end of his patience.

He received Dermot warily, and said that Lord Sandiford was out of Town. He had gone into the country for a few days and Mr. Todmore did not care to hazard a guess as to when he might return. He shook his head regretfully at Dermot's proffered guinea. "No, sir, it's not that. I really don't know, though happy to meet with a gentleman that's so ready to sport his blunt." He hesitated briefly, then said diffidently, "If it's a matter of a debt, sir, you're not the only one. If I may make so bold as to advise you, it might be better to have recourse to the law."

Dermot grinned, but shook his head. "Not that kind of debt. Let us say rather that I have a score to settle."

Mr. Todmore's expression of polite interest turned to one of dismay. "If it's a mill you have in mind, sir, this is my house and my furnishings. I want neither scandal nor damage, as I'll thank you to remember."

Dermot said soothingly that he would certainly endeavour to bear this point in mind. "You will be seeing me again," he promised. "I shall call upon his Lordship daily until I am so fortunate as to find him at home. Meanwhile—the truth is worth a good deal more than a pleasant lie," and he extended two guineas which this time found a readily receptive palm.

Frustrated in his primary aim, he spent a rather boring day, heartily wishing himself back at the Priory if he could have ensured that Katherine would be at his side. He had almost made up his mind to give pride the go-by and to lay his case before her. Or would it be better to approach her father first? It would certainly be more correct. But that meant two or three days out of Town, and he was anxious to settle his unfinished business with Lord Sandiford. After a period of sober reflection he decided that this must be his first concern. He had some no-

tion of being able to present Mr. Martenhays
with at least one sound reason for giving his
consent to so unequal a match for his daughter.
Dermot Winfield would know very well how to
take good care of his wife. She would run no
such horrid risks as she had experienced at Sandiford's hands. And to be able to add that the
offender had been brought to book must sub-
stantially strengthen his case.

Having decided so much, he spent the next
twenty four hours in mounting frustration. He
decided against paying a formal call on his beloved. She would be strictly chaperoned, and
what could he say to her under such circumstances that would advance his cause? Moreover
she might still be labouring under a sense of
obligation to him. It would be better to allow
time for her disproportionate gratitude to abate
a little. He might hope to meet her at Lady
Selby's *ridotto* that night, when there might be
a chance of fixing his interest with her in more
open and sociable circumstances. Meanwhile he
must find some means of passing the weary
hours, his early call on Lord Sandiford having
again gone unrewarded. His Lordship was still
out of Town, said Mr. Todmore sympathetically,
and had sent no message to herald his return.
Though that was only to be expected. It was his
way to come and go at will.

The slow passage of the empty hours put Mr.
Winfield in mind of a matter that had irked him

ever since his arrival in Town. At the Priory he had never felt the lack of a smart sporting vehicle such as a curricle or a whisky. His light travelling chaise was essential for necessary business or the occasional visit to Town, and the gig was perfectly adequate for his local journeyings if there were goods or implements to be transported. Otherwise he preferred to ride. But he had been bitterly jealous every time that he had seen Sandiford driving his dashing turnout in the Park with Katherine as his passenger. He himself was obliged to drive the lady in a hired vehicle, drawn by such commoners as the livery stable could supply. It was time that these shortcomings were remedied. Riding with the lady was all very well, and since she still preferred a quiet mount his livery hack was well able to keep abreast of hers; but opportunities for conversation were far more limited when one was riding, even in the restricted fashion permitted in the Park, than when seated side by side in a curricle or phaeton. A phaeton, decided Dermot, would be an absolute necessity if one were a married man. A curricle was scarcely suitable for a lady driver, but a phaeton, provided it was not of exaggerated design, would be perfectly proper. He indulged a happy little dream of teaching Katherine to tool such a vehicle about the quiet lanes converging on the Priory, and betook himself to Longacre, where he beguiled the afternoon pleasantly enough in inspecting the elegant carriages that were being offered, and in contemplating such additional luxuries as would make them fit for Katherine's use.

There were two vehicles that especially took his eye. One had the body mounted on elliptic springs, thus doing away with the need for a perch, and making a neat, light-weight model that would be easy for a lady to handle. The other, more conventional, with perch and cee springs, appealed to him for its colour. He laughed at himself for being swayed by such a triviality, and wondered if there was any limit to the folly of a man in love. Naturally he could have any carriage that he finally selected painted and picked out to his own—or Katherine's—taste. This one chanced to be the exact shade of deep blue that reminded him of a certain sapphire pendant.

He did not place a firm order. To do so might influence fortune against him, but he dropped a hint that there was a lady whose tastes would have to be consulted, and no consideration of the needs of the Priory was permitted to influence either his choice or his selection of desirable embellishments. Both he and the representative of Hatchetts were very well pleased with each other, and parted amicably in anticipation of a more decisive meeting at an early date.

It was three days before Lord Sandiford re-

turned to Town. The waiting did nothing to cool
his opponent's wrath. If anything it intensified
it, since the delay obliged him to defer matters
of vital importance. He managed to secure only
one dance with Katherine at Lady Selby's *ridotto* and by mutual consent they spoke solely
of trivial matters. There was no reference at all
to their midnight adventure. And although he
was so fortunate as to secure a seat beside her
during the musical part of the entertainment,
good manners forbade anything beyond the
most desultory remark while it was in progress.
He would have liked to invite her to ride with
him next day, but his eagerly awaited meeting
with Lord Sandiford must take pride of place.
In fact the evening left Katherine in a fit of the
dismals. She wondered anxiously if the adventure that they had shared had given Mr. Winfield a disgust of her. He had seemed quiet and
withdrawn, and had made no attempt at pro-
moting a further meeting.

Dermot, for his part, called on Lord Sandiford
at the indecently early hour of ten o'clock on
Friday morning, on the fret with impatience,
and cherishing a notion that his quarry might
have returned to his lodging late on the pre-
ceding evening, and would yet give him the slip
by an early departure. He was admitted by Mr.
Todmore, who did not wait for his enquiry but
favoured him with a significant nod. As Dermot
started impetuously for the stairs, however, he

put out a restraining hand and beckoned him mysteriously into his own small sanctum.

"His Lordship returned last night, sir," he announced as soon as he had closed the door. "He is now packing his gear for a prolonged stay with friends. It is fortunate that you called early today, or your business with him might have had to wait indefinitely. Perhaps you will announce yourself. I find that I have to go out on an errand. The door at the head of the stair—and pray remember my interest in the matter!"

He withdrew discreetly to the basement regions, leaving Dermot to make his own way to Lord Sandiford's apartment on the first floor. Mr. Todmore had no desire to be involved in the fracas that he anticipated, and a strategical withdrawal was the simplest method of achieving his purpose. He put on his hat and left the house by the area steps. As he trod briskly down the street, he observed two soberly dressed individuals coming towards him. So far as he was aware he had never seen either of them before, but experience had made him knowledgeable. He would have been willing to wager a modest sum that they were tipstaves, and that their destination was Lord Sandiford's lodging. Well—they would go empty away, since there was no one to admit them to the house. He walked on, untroubled by any qualms of conscience. Undoubtedly they would be back.

Dermot, receiving no response to his increas-

ingly imperative assaults on Lord Sandiford's
door knocker, finally lost patience. He knew
perfectly well that the fellow was within and
this was no time for paying undue heed to eti-
quette. He flung open the door and strode in.

It was a comfortably furnished apartment of
decent size, lit by two tall windows, and might
have presented an attractive appearance had it
not been in such disorder. A handsome walnut
bureau stood open against one wall, its drawers
pulled out crookedly to reveal the mass of papers
with which they were stuffed. A welter of dis-
carded garments was heaped on the chair, while
a driving coat, a hat, gloves and whip had been
flung on the floor. Across the room an open door
gave access to his Lordship's bedroom, which
was in a similar state of chaos. Two open valises
stood on the bed. His Lordship had been surprised in the homely task of packing his own
linen. His long-suffering valet, who had recieved no wages for the past year, had found
other employment, and departed without notice,
pointing out that he was well within his rights
in so doing. His Lordship, faced with the un-
accustomed task of doing his own packing, for
an indefinte stay in foreign parts, was making
heavy weather of it.

Hearing his door open, he came to the com-
municating doorway and said irritably, "What
is it now, Todmore? I thought I told you that"—

and broke off abruptly as he recognised his visitor.

From the description that Miss Keane had given him, he had a pretty good notion as to the identity of the stranger who had spirited Katherine away from the Grey Goose Feathers, and Dermot's unceremonious entrance confirmed every suspicion. His instinct was to put a good face on it, smooth things over. But he had more urgent preoccupations. Delay now was dangerous. He must get rid of this untimely visitor as quickly as possible.

"I did not hear your knock," he said, in his most insolent manner and without any pretence at greeting.

"Then you must be devilish hard of hearing," retorted Dermot curtly. "Not too deaf, I trust, to hear what I have to say to you."

"I'll listen if I must, you damned meddling marplot. But make it brief. I am in haste to be gone."

"That I can well understand," agreed Dermot suavely, "but there are debts to be settled first."

Lord Sandiford winced.

"Had it not been for the risk of scandal staining an innocent girl's name," Dermot went on, "it would not have been I who called upon you, but my friends. And you would not have escaped with the light punishment of a mere thrashing, which I propose to administer here and now. Give me leave to tell you, milord, that your deal-

Mira Stables

ings with Miss Martenhays must disgust any decent man, and that since her father is unable to bring you to book, it is for me, as his friend, to administer the necessary punishment."

"Don't be too sure of that," retorted his Lordship, anger making him forgetful of his pressing need for a swift departure; and beginning to struggle out of his coat. "I am not without experience in the manly art. It will be interesting to see which one gets the thrashing." He tossed the coat on to an already overloaded chair, causing a pile of garments to descend on to the floor, and began to roll up his sleeves in a businesslike way.

It was a question that was destined to remain unanswered. As Dermot squared up to him, purposefully, the door of the living room opened once more and two more uninvited guests walked into the room. They came rather diffidently but with a certain air of determination. Even in their profession it was not usual to enter a man's house without giving warning of their intention. But Mr. Todmore, in his haste to be gone after he had admitted Dermot, had neglected to close the street door, and the sight of it standing ajar had proved too much for the bailiffs to resist. It was a positive invitation to come to grips with the elusive Lord Sandiford, whom they had been seeking for several weary weeks.

The sight of their quarry banished any qualms

that they might have felt about the illicit nature of their entry, and they advanced boldly upon the two contestants.

"A mill!" proclaimed the shorter of the pair in gleeful surprise. "Well, I was always one for a good mill, and this pair look pretty well matched. What d'you say, Jos? Now that we've found his Lordship, our business with him may very well keep for a little while."

But his companion was made of sterner stuff.

"Your business may keep, Charley. Mine won't. I've been waiting to execute this 'ere warrant the best part o' three week, and no mill is going to stop me now. 'Oo's to say 'e wouldn't make an opportunity to slip out o' the room while we was all taken up wiv the fight? A fine dance he could lead us, for I doubt 'e's got the 'eels of both of us if it came to a chase. No. I'm for doing my dooty without delay," and he laid a magisterial, if slightly grimy, hand on his Lordship's arm, and cleared his throat portentously.

It was at this point that Dermot intervened. Unused as he was to dealings with writs and debt collectors, it had taken him a moment or two to appreciate the full possibilities of the situation. It was disappointing to be obliged to forego his personal vengeance, but it certainly looked as though he could safely leave Lord Sandiford's immediate future in the capable hands of Jos and Charlie. He could scarcely be expected to feel any sympathy for the wretched debtor, trapped in the toils of his own reckless folly; but one faint hint of fellow feeling remained. Despite his still simmering wrath at the treatment meted out to Katherine, he could spare Lord Sandiford the humiliation of having his rival see him haled off to prison.

He said politely, "Under the circumstances, milord, I suggest that we settle our differences at some future date. I will leave you to the entertainment of your new visitors, and will bid you au revoir."

FOURTEEN

Mr. Winfield wasted no time in returning to the Priory and going to call on Katherine's Papa. His dealings with Lord Sandiford had prevented him from dwelling at length on the possible course of an interview devoted to so important and delicate a business. On this homeward journey he did give a good deal of thought to his approach to Mr. Martenhays, but never got beyond the opening periods of his speech because so much depended on his listener's reaction. When he considered how he should go on if Mr. Martenhays rejected his appeal out of hand, he found himself wholly at a standstill. Katherine was of age, it was true, but Dermot, appreciating the deep affection between father and daughter, doubted if he could woo the girl in despite of her father's objections. She was a gentle creature. To be torn between father and lover would hurt her sorely. He could only hope that his recent services would incline Mr. Martenhays favourably towards him, and that a willingness to be patient—which went sadly against the grain—might eventually persuade that genial but irascible gentleman to consent to his suit.

It was heartening, then, to be given a welcome that vied with that accorded to the Prodigal Son. Mr. Martenhays did not exactly send his servants scurrying to provide every possible comfort for his unexpected guest, but there could be no mistaking his satisfaction in seeing him. He voiced it himself.

"Never so pleased to see any one in my life. Have you been down to your mill yet? They had the wheel running yesterday for the first time. Good progress they've made, despite your desertion. But it's a proper man, they say, whose fellows stick to the task he's set them without him breathing down their necks all the time. Still, you must be longing to see for yourself. Did you come down post? Then it'll do you good to stretch your legs and catch a breath of fresh air. Shall we go?"

So great was his enthusiasm that they were half way to the new mill before he remembered to ask after Katherine. He partly excused him-

self by explaining that he had recieved a letter
from her only that morning, but Dermot did not
feel that the moment was appropriate for an
intimate approach.

Striding along beside his friend, he managed
to break into the flow of enthusiasm for long
enough to suggest that after visiting the mill Mr.
Martenhays should come on to the Priory and
take pot-luck with him; when he would undertake to bring him up to date with his daughter's
progress, and such other items of Town news as
might prove of interest. Mr. Martenhays agreeing that they would both be ready for a bite by
the time that they had dealt faithfully with the
mill, and that certainly the Priory was more conveniently placed for their refreshment, the matter was amicably settled, and they were able to
devote the whole of their attention—or, in Dermot's case, a part of it—to such vital matters as
the height of the dam, the fall of water going over
the wheel, and the amount of machinery that it
might be expected to drive.

So absorbed was Mr. Martenhays in these
calculations that it seemed as though Dermot
would never find an opportunity to turn the conversation into the channel that he desired. Even
the excellent meal, supplied by a rather flurried
Hilda, taken by surprise by her master's unexpected return, and now faced with an extra
guest, did not stop the enthusiast. Between
mouthfuls he discoursed cheerfully on the great

mills of the North; not to be compared with this
small enterprise, of course, and vastly profitable
to their owners.

"At a vast cost in human misery," returned
Dermot soberly. "Which is partly what I had
in mind when I planned this one. I daresay it
will not be very profitable, though I trust it
will not run actually at a loss; but if will create
much needed employment here, in the countryside, instead of herding the people into those
grimy towns where the sun never seems to
shine. I went to school in the North and I have
seen something of them. Indeed it was the
memory of the many small mills on the banks
of some of the Lancashire rivers that gave me
the idea for this one—though they, of course,
are mostly cotton spinning mills."

Mr. Martenhays chewed thoughtfully, considering this confession with suitable gravity.
There was a faint air of diffidence about him
as he replied, "No reason why you should not
show a respectable profit, but you need a business head to run the thing. Wouldn't mind
having a touch at it myself, and you could
trust me not to grind the faces of the poor. Put
in a bit of capital, too. Tell you what, my dear
fellow, if you were to think of taking in a
partner, I hope you'll give me the first refusal."

This presented Dermot with the opportunity
that he had been seeking ever since his arrival.
"You are very good, sir," he said warmly. "To

be associated with you could bring nothing but pleasure and satisfaction. Perhaps we can consider the matter at our leisure. At the moment I have a much more vital business to put before you. Perhaps I am in the wrong that I plan to broach it under my roof, rather than under yours, but I can only plead that my impatience will brook no more delay."

Mr. Martenhays pricked up his ears hopefully. This was more like it—could surely only mean one thing.

"You have my full attention," he assured.

This was as well, for the story was long and involved. It began with the dismissal of the tinkers, when Dermot had first recognised in Katherine the girl of the Priory tapestry. It even admitted to some small annoyance with her conduct at that stage in the affair, and then went on to speak simply of his growing affection for her, as their acquaintance developed, and came thus to the nub of the matter with his decision that he could not speak of marriage to an heiress.

Mr. Martenhays uttered a disapproving grunt at this point, but Dermot then went on to explain the reasons that had taken him to London, which produced a more benevolent air in his listener, who felt that he could claim at least part of the credit for that very reasonable move.

Here the story suddenly faltered. Dermot had meant to tell of the course of events in Town, leading up to and including Katherine's abduction, feeling that this might well influence John Martenhays in his favour; but suddenly it struck him as a mean trick to play on an honest friendly fellow. He would win his bride by fair means. If Martenhays refused his consent, he would tell him straight out that Katherine was of age and that he planned to approach her directly. After all, if she loved him as he loved her, neither money nor filial devotion should be allowed to separate them.

He said abruptly, "Events in London tended to justify my action, but that is a long story and may well keep until we have settled a much more important matter. In Town, sir, I came to know your daughter even more intimately than had been possible here. We were for ever meeting at parties of different kinds. I grew to love her so much that my scruples about the inequality of our fortunes seemed less vital. At any cost I want her for my wife, and I humbly beg your permission to pay my addresses to her."

Mr. Martenhays did not keep him in suspense. "For my part," he said promptly, "I know no man I'd rather give her to. Though for a sensible fellow you talk a deal of rubbish. So—your fortune does not match mine. And neither does your age. By the time you are sixty turned, who's to say that you won't be a regular Midas or Croesus, or whoever the fellow was, that was so well inlaid? You're willing to work and to deny yourself luxuries in order to cherish your estates. That's the style for my taste. I once told you that I couldn't abide Sandiford because he was an expensive idler, and that such a one would never do for my prudent Katherine. It wasn't just because his pockets were to let. That wouldn't have mattered if he'd tried to bring himself about. But so far as I could see, all he thought of was dipping his fingers into my coffers; which is as near stealing as makes no odds, even if you do dignify it by talking of marriage settlements. You, on the other hand, appear to be well able to support a wife in modest comfort, which is all that she has the right to ask. Some day in the future—the distant future, I trust—Katherine will inherit the bulk of my fortune. But to permit that distant prospect to hold you back from making the girl an offer, is the kind of high-minded folly that I have no patience with. I respect you the more for putting it aside."

Dermot heaved a sigh of relief. It was vastly comforting to have his motives so well understood. He pushed the decanter towards his guest. "Your glass is empty, sir. Let us drink to the hope of a closer alliance between us."

"As to that, I always said we should be in partnership," retorted Mr. Martenhays, recharging his glass. "Both in farming matters, and now in this mill business of yours. And, as

I say, there's no man to whom I'd rather entrust my daughter. But the final word doesn't rest with us. Katherine is a good, biddable daughter, but in such an important matter I wouldn't try to persuade her against her will. If she likes you well enough, then you may take her with my blessing. But it will be for her to decide."

As though there was any doubt about it, Mr. Martenhays thought amusedly, and the pair of them smelling of April and May for weeks before Katherine's sudden flight to Town. Some lovers' tiff, that, he supposed, now happily composed.

He sipped his wine. "But you were to tell me of your dealings with Lord Sandiford," he remembered. "I take it that he resented your interference."

"He did not show it," acknowledged Dermot. "On the surface we were amazingly cordial. Though neither of us missed an opportunity to taking the wind out of the other's eye."

Mr. Martenhays grinned. The notion of his daughter holding herself delicately aloof while the two contending warriors sparred for her favour could not but please him.

This mood of jovial complacency was shattered by Dermot's account of the abduction of his daughter, and the plot to force her into marriage with Lord Sandiford. His brow grew thunderous, and, once he had accepted the shocking truth, his questions came abrupt and trenchant.

An abstemious man, he refilled his glass again and yet again, as he listened, and was deeply concerned to learn how the rescue had been effected so smoothly, and the danger of a resounding scandal averted. When the tale was done he relapsed into a brooding silence that lasted several minutes. Dermot, respecting his mood, awaited the verdict quietly.

It came with characteristic honesty. "I have not guarded the girl as I should. Selfish to leave her so much to Julia, kind and careful as she is. Sandiford and others of his kidney might reasonably conclude that I was not overconcerned with my girl's happiness. I should have opened up the house in Arlington Street as soon as she made her come out. Julia could easily have been persuaded to live with us until such time as Katherine chose to marry; and my fatherly care for my child would have been apparent to all. I did not give enough weight to such considerations, being too taken up with my agricultural toys, and am sadly at fault."

"Katherine does not think so, sir," assured Dermot comfortingly. "She said you might scold her for being too naive and trusting, and for being taken in by a knave, but she told me herself that if I had not come to her rescue she could have relied absolutely upon your support. 'I would never have yielded,' she said. 'I would never have consented to marriage with him.

And my father would have been the first to support me in that decision.' She knew that she could perfectly rely upon you, sir, so there is no reason to blame yourself."

"That's my Katherine," acknowledged Mr. Martenhays quietly. "A generous creature. But her generosity does not absolve me from blame— nor make me backward in acknowledging my debt to you."

Words failed him. He thrust out a hand and clasped Dermot's in a painful grip. "I will not try to say it, lad, but if ever I can serve you in any way, you have only to ask. As for a marriage between you and Katherine, it is, as I said, for her to decide. But I shall be the first to rejoice in such a union, if it can be agreed. And now may we stop harrowing up our emotions and revert to practical matters? It is in my mind to go with you when you go up to Town. Or rather not with you, where I suspect that I should be deucedly in the way, but at the same time. I shall go to Arlington Street, and if you and Katherine settle affairs comfortably between you, you will know where to find me. And I shall be in a position to arrange matters smoothly for an early wedding. If that is your desire," he finished, with a teasing twinkle.

FIFTEEN

The last of the Season's big 'squeezes' thought Katherine, studying her reflection in the mirror, as her maid set the diamond circlet on her carefully dressed hair. Her mood was one of resignation rather than of festive eagerness. Of course she must go to the party, converse, laugh, perhaps even flirt a little. The social whirl could not be expected to come to a halt because one insignificant girl was in low spirits.

She dismissed her maid, and yielded wholly to her dismal reflections. In three days' time she would be going home again. And what had her flight from home achieved? Only confirmation of the knowledge that she was hopelessly in love with Dermot Winfield. And he? Once or twice she had ventured to hope that he showed a certain partiality for her society. Probably that was just because he felt at ease with her, and reckoned her father as his very good friend. Their talk was not entirely limited to topics acceptable to the *ton*. They could speak of the Priory and of Hays Park; even of the new mill that Dermot was having built. Probably Mr. Winfield found such talk a refreshing change from the artificialities of social chatter. She had almost convinced herself that it was no more than that, especially since they had shared that midnight adventure. She had indulged the hope that it would serve to draw them closer together, but instead, she had scarcely set eyes on him since he had brought her back to Lady Julia. Certainly she had never thanked him properly for the tremendous service that he had rendered her. But how could she have done so in the middle of a formal party? The only time that she had been able to exchange a few words with him had been at the Selby's *ridotto*. And now he was gone out of Town.

She and Lady Julia had received an unusually large number of morning callers that day, all eager to canvas every aspect of the shocking news of Lord Sandiford's apprehension for debt. There had been avid curiosity, and a certain degree of malice, in some of the remarks that were addressed to Katherine. She had striven to preserve a mildly interested and sympathetic front, saying that the event was not wholly unexpected, and trusting that his lordship would find some means of compounding with his creditors that would permit of his early release. To speak truth, she actually did feel a little sorry for him. Whatever he had purposed against her, he had been completely outmanoeuvred, and she still found it difficult to believe that Julian, her laughing, light-hearted cavalier, would ever really have meant to hurt her. And at least he had been loyal in one respect. No mention of her discreditable adventure had got about. By now, it would have been easy enough to read the signs if that had happened. But no. Her social life ran as smoothly as ever, if only one could be rid of these sensation hunters who were all so eager to probe her reaction to poor Sandiford's troubles.

It was one of them, a Mrs. Swann—whose daughter, alas, no swan, but very much an ugly duckling, consistently outshone by Katherine— who let fall the news that Mr. Winfield had gone out of Town.

"Excused himself from the Garnett's rout last night on the plea of urgent business at home. I'm sure I'm not surprised. The only wonder is that he had lingered so long. The first time in all the years I've known him."

Katherine might have taken some comfort from this, but Mrs. Swann was not done with her. "You will scarcely know how to fill your programme tonight, Miss Martenhays, with both your regular beaux missing. Though I daresay it will be easier for a young lady of your standing"—her expression breathed the word 'expectations'—"than it would be for such as my poor Amabel who is so painfully shy."

Since that was not Katherine's opinion of Miss Swann, whom she thought pushing and at times insolent, she was able to restrain her sympathies. She returned a pleasantly non-committal answer, and was thankful when the last caller departed, acknowledging, however, that there had been a good deal of truth in Mrs. Swann's taunt about wondering how to fill the gaps in her programme. It was with no particular expectation of enjoyment that she presently drew her cloak about her shoulders, ready to join Aunt Julia in the hall.

Sometimes, when that eventful night was done, she wondered superstitiously if her choice of dress and jewellery had done anything to influence its course. Surely not? It had been simple common sense to try to raise her spirits by wearing a new dress. Only it had been a dress of blue silk that made her eyes look blue, and reminded her insistently of the sapphire pendant. She hesitated only briefly. Why not? It might well be her last opportunity of wearing the charming jewel. This was the last big party of the Season, and she did not think that she would return to Town next year. Nor would she

venture to wear it at home where Mr. Winfield
might see it. Tonight he would not be there. The
pendant matched her dress so beautifully,
adorned the plain neck-line, and went well with
the circlet of diamonds in her hair. It was the
work of a moment to clasp it round her throat,
pull up her cloak to hide it from Aunt Julia's
enquiring interest, and scurry down to the hall,
suddenly armoured with some sort of secret
courage, almost as though the pendant was a
talisman that would help her to endure an evening of considerable social discomfort.

It turned out to be better than she had expected. No gathering from which Dermot was
absent could be completely satisfactory, but the
party was a very successful one, given by one
of Society's most popular hostesses. A normal
healthy girl could not wholly resist the lilt of
the music, the smiling faces of her friends, the
careless greetings exchanged with passing couples. She had plenty of partners, too, in spite of
Mrs. Swann's gloomy warning. The blue dress
suited her to admiration, and if her expression
was a little lacking in animation she held her
head high and behaved with her usual pretty
dignity. There were plenty of gentlemen happy
enough to secure so pleasant a partner, and one
or two who even wondered if she might turn her
eyes towards them, now that Sandiford was out
of the running.

These burgeoning hopes were doomed to dis-
appointment. It was fortunate that Katherine

had just reached the bottom of the set before she recognised the tall familiar figure bowing over his hostess's hand. She was able to notice that he spent a few minutes in conversation with that lady—apologising, perhaps, for his tardy arrival—without losing her place in the figures; but try as she would she could no longer focus all her attention on either her partner or the demands of the dance. She got through the rest of it mechanically, her eyes ever alert for the whereabouts of the beloved figure. Would he ask her to dance? She was promised for the next two dances. The most that she could hope for was that he and his partner might join the same set, and that gave little opportunity for conversation.

The dance ended. She thanked her partner for the pleasure it had given her, and permitted him to restore her to Lady Julia's side, and to supply her with a glass of champagne cup. He stayed chatting with them for a few moments before going off in search of his new partner. Mr. Winfield bowed before Katherine. Since he had approached from behind the rows of chairs where the chaperones had established themselves, she had not seen him coming, and her colour rose in betraying fashion. He greeted Lady Julia before turning his attention to her charge.

"May I venture to hope that I am not come

too late to claim the privilege of dancing with Miss Martenhays?" he said gently.

Katherine replied suitably, her voice steady, though her hands shook a little. They settled it that they would dance the first quadrille together.

"And perhaps you would sup with me," continued Dermot smoothly. "I am told that supper will be served during both sets of quadrilles; so if you are not yet engaged for the second set, we could recover from our exertions while we sup."

Lady Julia raised a delicate eyebrow. The first quadrille and supper to follow. It was not precisely fast, but such attentions were distinctly marked. He must mean to come to the point. Well—she was all in favour. She made no demur when Katherine said in a breathless little voice that that would be very agreeable.

So far as Katherine was concerned the next two dances were dream-like. The rigid training of the years stood her in good stead, for she played her part competently enough, even though her heart seemed to be beating somewhere in her throat, and her mind to be confusion of hope and doubt. Perhaps the champagne cup helped, too, for she chattered gaily, if inconsequentially, with her partners, and never had she been in better looks. Even her jealous critics admitted that blue became her. It seemed to make her eyes look larger and more brilliant; while the pretty colour coming and going in her cheeks made her seem more softly feminine.

She and her partner performed the first quadrille, with due attention paid to the figures. This apparently left them with little scope for conversation, for they exchanged only one or two brief remarks. Dermot was a little more talkative over supper, telling her of his visit to the Priory, and reporting that he had left her father in good health and spirits. Oddly enough, he forgot to mention that he had left him in Arlington Street and not at Hays Park. Neither the lady nor the gentleman appeared to have much appetite for the delicious viands that were spread before them, Katherine nibbling languidly at a chicken patty and apricot tartlets; Dermot saying that having dined late he was not in the least hungry. Presently he suggested that his companion might care to stroll in the conservatory for a while. Surely there, he thought, he might find a secluded corner where he could talk to the girl without fear of interruption. There would be other people about, it was true, but with the second set of quadrilles in progress and the supper room fairly crowded, they would not be very many. Katherine, agreeing in a stiff little voice that the notion was a good one, rose to accompany him.

After the brilliant illuminations in the ballroom and supper room, the conservatory seemed quite dark, though even here coloured lanterns had been disposed about the banks of greenery, to give a soft glow of light. Dermot suggested that Katherine should take his arm lest she stumble in the uncertain light. She did so, and the touch of that soft little hand suddenly revived his impatience and frustration. He laid his free hand over it, and said abruptly, "Miss Martenhays—Katherine, dear Katherine. I cannot say all that is in my heart, for someone is bound to come and interrupt us before I have half done. Only let me say that it is my most earnest desire to marry you. I have your father's permission to approach you on this head. This must come as a great shock to you, for no doubt you have thought of me only as a friend and neighbour—if you thought about me at all. I cannot say when my own feelings changed from liking to love. It happened so naturally that I was swept away before I realised. If I had realised, I must have tried to set a sterner guard upon my feelings, since I already knew how you felt about marriages between persons of disproportionate fortune. You told me of your views, you may recall, when we were talking of Emma Dorsey; and on several occasions since then, you have shown only too plainly how you felt about fortune hunters. Small use to say that I do not want your fortune, though it would be true. It is true also to say that you are the only girl with whom I can happily contemplate spending the rest of my life. But could you so contemplate spending all your days with me? As you know, the Priory is no more than a modest manor. Could you face life as the wife of a plain land-owner, with neither wealth, title nor splendid estates, but only a great deal of hard work and making shift to stretch every penny to the ut-most?"

The small hand turned confidingly under his, so that their fingers interlaced. "You offer me a kingdom that I never dreamed to possess," said Katherine steadily. "I ask for nothing bet-ter than to work beside you, and to help stretch the pence. All my life I have only had to ask for anything that I desired. Things too easily won are little valued. Happiness is not won that way. Working together, helping each other, I think that we shall be well content. I accept your offer, sir, and will be proud and happy to become your wife."

Dermot would have folded her in his arms and kissed the soft appealing mouth, but at that moment another couple strolled towards them. He could only crush the slender fingers en-trusted to his, in a speaking fashion that left them tingling for a quarter of an hour; and sug-gest politely that they should return to the ball-room.

The rest of the evening passed in a haze of happiness for Katherine. She danced, chatted, laughed, and glowed with happiness, so that Lady Julia smiled contentedly, and awaited, with the deepest interest, the revelations that would be forthcoming after the ball. Mr. Winfield, restoring her charge to her side after the supper interlude, had said only that he would do himself the honour of waiting upon her next day; and she could scarcely embark on a confidential talk with Katherine in the middle of a crowded ballroom, but she was convinced in her own mind that all was now happily settled. She wondered if Mr. Winfield had taken the precaution of asking Cousin John's consent before approaching his daughter. She thought it most probable that he had. For all his easy ways he was something of a stickler for convention. In a matter so important as a marriage he would be likely to observe all the proper forms.

Katherine was able to set her mind at rest on this and any other doubtful points, as they drove back from the party. Aunt Julia's curiosity could no longer be restrained, and the dim interior of the carriage was a tacit invitation to confidences. A deeply happy Katherine was eager to pour out all the details of the future that she and her betrothed were planning. It sounded surprisingly spartan to Lady Julia, but no doubt the lovers were in that frame of mind that thinks the world and all its luxuries well lost for love. She raised no objections. In the girl's present mood it would be a waste of breath. Once the knot was fairly tied, Cousin John would see to it that his daughter's husband came down from his high ropes, when it was a question of financial backing. She would have found it inconceivable that Cousin John not only knew all about Mr. Winfield's scruples, but actually liked him the better for them; or that that wily man of affairs had his own notions of the best way of dealing with a stiff-necked, high-principled son-in-law. A hint that he was growing older; that he could use the services and energies of a younger man to support him in his many dealings—and the partnership that he had mentioned once or twice would be fairly launched. It would not be easy. Dermot Winfield was no fool. But if Mr. Martenhays did not over-play his part or try to hurry things too much, the trick should hold.

Katherine woke early next day, even though she had not sought her bed until three o'clock. She woke to that sense of delight that promises something pleasant in the immediate future, even before one is fully awake, and stretched luxuriously beneath the covers as she recalled the conversation with Dermot on the previous evening, but she felt much too full of life and energy to play slug-a-bed. She rang for her maid and proceeded to dress, choosing a plain morning gown of figured muslin, made high to the throat and trimmed with a single ruffle, and round her neck she clasped the sapphire pendant. It was not at all the thing to wear jewellery in the morning, but for once she was pre-

pared to defy convention. Soon, perhaps, she
thought joyously, she would wear Dermot's betrothal ring. Until then she would wear his pendant.

She loitered over her breakfast in an attempt
to fill in the time of waiting; arranged fresh
bowls of flowers for the hall and drawing room,
and tried to interest herself in a new novel from
the circulating library, but the very minutes
seemed endless. Eventually, even the sympathetic Lady Julia was fretted by her fidgets and
asked if she could not find some needlework to
occupy her restless fingers. And when the long
awaited visitor was announced, both ladies
were surprised. For he was not alone. Mr. Martenhays came with him, smiling broadly at their
startled faces, bestowing a crushing hug on his
daughter as he stooped to kiss her cheek, and
informing her, before she regained breath enough
to welcome him, that she was a good little puss
and that he was very pleased with her. In case
she was in any doubt as to the source of his
satisfaction, he then slapped Dermot on the
shoulder and added bluntly, "I never did care
for that spendthrift Sandiford, let alone his
scandalous behaviour towards you last week.
Yes, I know all about it, and whom I have to
thank that you came off safely and without talk.
I've small use for all these romantic tales that
you females set such store by, but it seems to
me only right and proper that your rescuer

should recieve your hand in marriage. However, he tells me that it's no such thing. He was tail over top in love with you—has been these six months past—and only the thought of your money-bags put him off. Which I must say is a new come-out in my experience. However, I've assured him that I don't mean to pop off the hooks for years to come, and that if he wants you he must take you with just the allowance that I settled on you when you came of age. I hope I did right, child. At least it appeased his scruples and gave him the courage to pop the question."

The speaker's careless joviality was masterly. No one hearing him could have discerned the first steps in his campaign to overcome Dermot's prejudice against fortune hunting. Katherine was not sufficiently awake to the time of day to realise that her generous allowance had never actually been settled on her. She would never think to question it, and Dermot would accept her acceptance. He must make a point of getting the whole thing neatly tied up the very next day, decided Mr. Martenhays. Meanwhile his listeners appeared to have swallowed his pretty fable without a blink.

He was careful not to labour the point, going on to speak at length of his pleasure in the betrothal, and his hope that the wedding would not be too long delayed.

Modesty compelled Katherine to restrain the

suggestion that it could not be too soon. Dermot was eager to claim his bride, Lady Julia concerned with all the preparations that would be necessary for a fashionable wedding. Katherine and her father were unanimous in their rejection of this proposal. After some lively discussion, all four agreed on a September wedding in the village church where Katherine had been baptised. It was small—but they were not planning a large function with hordes of guests who meant nothing to either of the contracting parties.

"Plenty of room for our real friends and for the folk from the estates," pronounced Mr. Martenhays. And Lady Julia was brought to agree that September was a very good month for a farmer to marry—if the harvest weather had been favourable—and that the village church was conveniently situated, both for Hays Park and the Priory.

That settled, Mr. Martenhays turned to Lady Julia. "Do you think, while I am here, that you could lay your hand on the lease of this house? A rumour has reached me that it may be possible to buy the freehold. I would like to do so, but first I must check the details in the lease. Particularly how many years are left to run."

Lady Julia assured him that she could do so without delay. He opened the door for her and followed her out of the room. It was careless of him not to assure himself that the latch had clicked home; so that the betrothed pair were perfectly well able to hear him say, "No particular hurry, my dear. Just wanted to give them a few minutes on their own. The boy tells me he proposed to her last night during the supper interval. Can't even have had a chance to kiss her—and after all these months of waiting. Give them quarter of an hour together."

The two listeners exchanged startled glances. Then Katherine's lips quivered into irresistible laughter. She held out both hands. Dermot swept her into his arms and proceeded to carry out the senior partner's instructions, with a devotion to duty that was quite admirable. Presently Katherine, rosy and breathless, pushed him away a little and said unsteadily, "And you don't think my father tight-fished to grudging when he says that I shall have only my allowance?"

"I was never more grateful to any one in my life," returned Dermot frankly. "His wealth was the one great barrier that stood between us. You, I was aware, dreaded being courted for your wealth. I, I confess, was too proud to accept the stigma of fortune hunting. As your father has arranged things we shall do very well. We shall have a full and busy life, which will suit both of us, and money sufficient for our modest needs."

She nodded vigorously, whereat he kissed her again and drew her down to sit beside him on the sofa, his arm about her shoulders, while they discussed that topic of such vital interest to lovers—the exact point in their acquaintance when each had realised the attraction of the other. Katherine declared that she had known her own mind these weeks past; that she had, in fact, fled Hays Park and come up to Town in an attempt to put him out of her thoughts.

"For you never showed any particular preference for me," she accused, "and I was determined that I would not wear the willow for you."

"I had not, at that time, persuaded myself that I was a fit match for you," he explained. "Nor have I yet. I only know that I cannot do without you, so you must just make the best of your bad bargain."

"You are the one who is getting the bad bargain," she said soberly. "I'm neither pretty nor gifted, and, if it had not been for you, I should not even have a fair reputation left to me. And I have never thanked you properly for rescuing me from that horrid inn."

His hold tightened at this reminder of the danger in which she had stood, but before he could speak she went on, "I can't think why you should make me an offer after that foolish escapade."

He tilted her chin gently, so that she was obliged to lift her face to his, and he realised from her sober expression that she was in deadly earnest.

"I'll not have you say such things about my promised wife," he told her, mock-severe. "You cannot judge of your own looks, for you do not see your face when it is animated. You will say that I am prejudiced, but it is the kind of face that a man wants to live with. It has warmth and charm, and when you are happy it is beautiful. Don't repine because it is not a painted pink and white mask. As for gifts"—he hugged her and laughed—"you oblige me to disclose my guilty secret. I can honestly declare that I was not interested in your father's money. But I did covet his daughter's companionship. Whenever I came to Hays Park, I was instantly at home. You never fussed or seemed put out, however odd the hour or the demands that your father and I made on your hospitality. And when you came to the Priory and helped me to plan the repairs and decorations you always seemed to be really interested, and your ideas were fresh and sensible. Economical, too. You have a gift for home making, my girl. It doesn't sound very romantic, does it? But I can assure you that it is a hundred times better than being able to play the harp or paint in water colours. You'll make your husband a contented man as well as a proud one. But don't be thinking that I only want you for your domestic talents. I want all of you. Your love and your tenderness. The impulsive generosity that even extends to a pack of useless tinkers. The comradeship that I have seen between you and your father—the way you share his interests even though they are not the kind that one would expect to appeal to a woman. Until you came into my life I did not know how lonely I was. Now I want to keep you with me all the time. You must always be there for me to come home to. It's not a fashionable marriage that I'm offering you, my little love, with both of us free to go our own ways, so think well before you surrender your freedom. I shall be a possessive husband, though not, I trust, a wholly selfish one."

Katherine gave a small ecstatic shiver. His words appealed to all her deepest instincts, confirmed her in the belief that they were meant for one another. He had not attempted to soothe her doubts by fobbing her off with pretty compliments. He had spoken the truth from his heart. She recognised it and was deeply satisfied. If she could have seen the face that she turned to him, she would have known that he had spoken truth there, too. Glorified by love, it was, indeed, beautiful.

She said simply, "I don't need more time to think. I need you every bit as much as you need me." She managed a rather wavering little smile. "Ever since our first meeting in the Priory stable you have been coming to my rescue. It was you who helped me get over my fear of horses, you who picked me up and took me home when Ajax threw me, who came to my help in that business with the tinkers. When I was abducted, who saved me from social ruin? It's plain to be seen that I can't do without you. And since the only way in which I can rely upon having you always at hand, to come to my rescue, is to marry you, then the sooner we can achieve that desirable state, the happier I shall be." She lifted one hand and gently touched his face, then held up her own to be kissed.